BEWILDERED IN BERLIN

From the library of

Name ______________________

Address ______________________

____

____

THE ROMANTIC NOVELS OF

BARBARA CARTLAND

BEWILDERED IN BERLIN

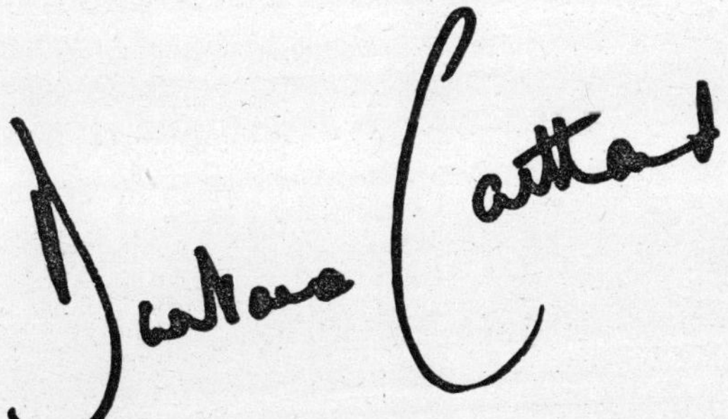

Eaglemoss Publications Limited
7 Cromwell Road
London SW7 2HR

First published 1986

Set in Sabon
Made and printed in Great Britain by
Richard Clay (The Chaucer Press) Ltd,
Bungay, Suffolk

ISBN 1 85167 076 9

BEWILDERED IN BERLIN

Although he would rather go to France, Lord Braydon is ordered by the Prince of Wales to go to Berlin to try and discover a 'secret weapon' it has been rumoured they have.

Once aboard the train he begins to settle down for the night when there is a knock on his door and a young girl stands there begging for his help.

Loelia has been frightened by a large German who has been pestering her and Lord Braydon arranges for her to change her sleeper for his valet's.

Following a dinner party in Berlin Lord Braydon is taken reluctantly to a Brothel where to his surprise he finds Loelia who has been kidnapped and drugged, and again he saves her.

Loelia tells him that she has come to Berlin to try and find her father who she is certain is being held captive somewhere and her intuition tells her that she can find him.

How Lord Braydon helps her once again and finds her father, how he discovers the secret the Prince of Wales is longing to be the first to hear and how in Loelia he finds perfect love is told in an exciting new book by Barbara Cartland.

AUTHOR'S NOTE

The animosity between the Prince of Wales, later King Edward VII, was exactly as I have described in this novel, when the Kaiser became what the Prince called 'the boss of Cowes'.

The Prince had always been the star of the annual Regatta, and was Commodore of the Royal Yacht Squadron, as well as of the Royal Thames Yacht Club and President of the Yacht Racing Association.

He was extremely proud that his own racing cutter, the *Britannia*, had won many an important race with him aboard. In fact he described it as "the finest racing yacht afloat".

In 1893 the Kaiser had spoiled all this when he appeared at Cowes with a new yacht of his own, '*Meteor I*', with which he beat the Prince in the Queen's Cup race.

In 1895 he antagonised the Regatta Committee by ostentatiously withdrawing '*Meteor I*' from the race on the grounds that the handicapping was unfair to him.

Before leaving Cowes that year, as I have explained in this book, the Kaiser approached George Lennox Watson, the designer of the 300 ton '*Britannia*', and ordered a yacht that would be even bigger and faster than '*Meteor I*'.

The Prince felt he could not cope with this. He sold '*Britannia*' in which he had taken such pride, and although he bought it back when he became King and thereafter attended Cowes with unfailing regularity, he never took part in a race there again.

The Queen's Cup was won by the Kaiser in 1899 with his unrivalled '*Meteor II*'.

CHAPTER ONE

1896

Lord Braydon boarded the train at Ostend which was to carry him to Berlin.

There was a frown between his eyes and an expression which told those who knew him well that he was in an extremely bad temper.

He had been in one ever since he had risen that morning.

He had to cross the Channel and set off on what he thought was a "Fool's errand" to Germany.

He disliked the Germans, although he had found a few who were tolerable.

He disliked even more being obliged to carry out the Prince of Wales' wishes when he knew they were bound to be abortive.

Three nights ago he had accompanied the Prince to the Royal Opera House at Covent Garden.

He had realised from the way His Royal Highness was looking at him that something untoward would happen before the end of the evening.

As usual, when the Prince attended the Opera, his arrival was preceded by a Chef and six footmen.

They carried with them numerous hampers filled with table-silver, gold plate and food.

A ten or twelve course meal was served in a room at the back of the box during the hour-long interval.

Lord Braydon, like many of his friends at Court, always found this slightly amusing.

At the same time, it certainly relieved the monotony of a long Opera when both the wine and the food were superlative.

At the end of the Opera when they returned to Marlborough House Lord Braydon was aware that the Prince was seeking an opportunity to speak to him.

It was impossible to leave before Princess Alexandra retired.

Lord Braydon had however hoped to slip away the moment her back was turned.

The Prince of Wales unfortunately prevented this.

"I want to speak to you, Braydon," he said.

It was intended to be a *sotto voce* aside, but was in fact overheard by the rest of the party.

They therefore made their farewells while Lord Braydon waited somewhat apprehensively behind.

He was a tall and extremely handsome man, much in demand.

Not only by the Prince of Wales, who was very fond of him, but also by a great number of beautiful women who successively held his attention for a short while.

In fact until he tired of each one.

The trouble with all his *affaires de coeur* was invariably the same.

It was that Lord Braydon became bored with what he thought of as "the monotony of the obvious".

He found himself longing for something original, something different.

At the same time he recognised he was asking too much of life when Fate had already been exceedingly generous to him.

He was the owner of an ancient title and he was extremely wealthy.

His ancestral home in Oxfordshire was one of the most spectacular and beautiful in England.

His racing-stable was admired and envied not only in his own country, but also in France.

His race-horses certainly gave him an excuse to visit

the gayest Capital in Europe regularly.

This was another reason why he was incensed.

An express for Paris was waiting at the docks for the passengers who had crossed the Channel from Dover to Folkestone.

Lord Braydon had himself crossed in his own yacht, which had arrived simultaneously with the Tilbury steamer.

This made his having to take the Berlin train even more irritating.

His valet, Watkins, who always travelled with him, saw that his luggage was carefully stowed in his sleeper.

He ordered the porter to convey anything that was not required by his Master on the journey into the compartment next door.

Because Lord Braydon wished to be comfortable he always insisted that his valet had a sleeping compartment next to his own.

This meant the man was at hand when he needed him, and that he would not be disturbed by passengers who talked loudly, or others who woke him during the night by slamming doors.

His friends had often commented that this was an extravagant arrangement, but Lord Braydon always replied by saying:

"There is nothing more important on which one should spend money than on one's own comfort."

Since this was really their outlook on life also it was impossible for them to complain.

As he tipped the porter generously on his Master's behalf, Watkins glanced round the compartment and said unnecessarily:

"I'm next door, M'Lord, if Your Lordship needs me."

Lord Braydon did not even bother to reply, he merely sat back in the seat which had not yet been made into a bed for the night.

He wondered how soon he could get away from Berlin.

He would then inform the Prince of Wales, as he was

quite certain he would have to do, that he had been unable to carry out his wishes.

In other words that his mission had been unsuccessful.

Only the Prince of Wales, Lord Braydon thought, could have conceived the absurd idea that he should try to discover from the Germans the exact extent of their new Naval armaments programme!

The Prince's relations with Germany had never been easy.

First came the trouble over his known sympathy to France during the Franco–Prussian war.

Then the Prince and his sister had encouraged the love-match of Prince Alexander of Battenburg with Princess Victoria, daughter of the Crown Prince of Prussia.

On top of all this, the Prince of Wales found Prince Wilhelm a tiresome young man who also offended Queen Victoria.

A visit to England had been vetoed with the result that Prince Wilhelm had remained in Germany.

There he made insulting remarks about his uncle, calling him 'a fat peacock' and had referred to his grandmother as 'an old hag'.

The Prince of Wales had, after that, ignored him.

In 1888, within a year of the Jubilee, Wilhelm had become the Kaiser at the age of twenty-nine.

The Prince of Wales had taken little trouble to disguise his dislike of the new Kaiser.

Nor did he guard his tongue when speaking of his nephew.

He talked of him as 'William the Great' and was infuriated when the Kaiser, very puffed up with his own importance, retaliated.

However despite the quarrel the Kaiser came to England in 1889 determined to be pleasant.

After that things were slightly better until he decided to become what the Prince called 'The Boss of Cowes'.

The Prince of Wales had always been the 'star' of the annual Regatta.

He was Commodore of the Royal Yacht Squadron and

his racing cutter, *'Britannia'* with himself aboard, had won many important races.

She was considered the finest racing yacht afloat.

But the Kaiser had spoiled all that by beating the Prince for the Queen's Cup.

He had afterwards set about using Cowes as a show-place for the latest warships of the German Navy.

Ths year before, in 1895, he had arrived in the Imperial yacht, *'Hohenzollern'* escorted by Germany's two newest warships *'Worth'* and *'Weissenburg'*.

They were named after German victories during the Franco–Prussian war.

He antagonized the Regatta committee by ostentatiously withdrawing his yacht from the race The Queen's Cup.

He declared that the handicapping was unfair to him.

He was then deliberately rude to his uncle at a dinner-party aboard the *'Osborne'*.

The Prince of Wales' fury was known to everybody in the Royal Household.

Lord Braydon was therefore not entirely surprised when the Prince said to him as soon as they were alone:

"I want you to do something for me, Braydon, which means going to Germany."

Lord Braydon drew in his breath, but he did not reply.

Walking up and down the room in an agitated fashion the Prince of Wales said:

"I've heard from quite an impeccable source, that my nephew the Kaiser has a new Naval gun which is more deadly and more effective than anything we have."

He paused for breath and as Lord Braydon still did not speak he went on:

"I know your brilliance at languages, and that you speak German like a native, so if anybody can find out what is going on it is you."

"I think that is very unlikely, Sir," Lord Braydon replied. "If it is as secret as you think, the Germans will guard it very effectively, and I could hardly expect them to talk to me about it."

"I want to know what it is," the Prince of Wales said obstinately, "We know they are building ships, but if these ships are armed with better guns than we ourselves can produce, then it might be really dangerous."

Lord Braydon knew that the Prince was convinced, like a great number of other people, that sooner or later Germany would challenge Britain's supremacy at sea.

It was well known that the Kaiser was extremely jealous of her far-flung Empire.

He talked openly of Germany acquiring more 'living space'.

Lord Braydon knew it was hopeless to argue. He merely said:

"I will go to Germany and do my best Sir, but I hope Your Royal Highness will not expect miracles."

The Prince made a sound but did not interrupt, and Lord Braydon continued:

"I very much doubt if I shall be able to bring you back any information which you do not already possess."

He intended this as a subtle compliment.

The Queen still kept her son in ignorance of all State papers.

The Prince was not allowed to take part in any important discussion, while he did everything he could to acquire the knowledge that was kept from him.

He liked to think he was 'in the know'.

Lord Braydon realised that if he could hear of some secret weapon before the Foreign Office or the British Naval authorities, it would definitely be a 'feather in his cap'.

The Prince put his hand on Lord Braydon's shoulder.

"I consider this very important, Braydon," he said "and I know how successful you have been on other missions which I had better not mention."

"Much better not, Sir!" Lord Braydon agreed hastily.

At times the Prince, especially when he was with a beautiful woman, was inclined to be indiscreet.

"You will leave at once?" the Prince enquired.

"The day after tomorrow," Lord Braydon promised.

He returned to his large and very comfortable house in Park Lane.

He vented his bad temper next day on his staff and to their surprise on a number of his friends.

He was in general somewhat aloof and inclined to be reserved.

He also had a self-control which made him seldom reveal his true feelings.

He could be amusing, witty, and, as the Prince of Wales knew, he was exceedingly intelligent.

But there were times when even those who knew him well and admired him thought him somewhat awe-inspiring.

Women, although they were fascinated by him, found him an enigma they did not pretend to understand.

"I love you, Oswin," one beautiful woman had said to him only a few days ago, "but I never feel that I know you really well."

"What do you mean by that?" Lord Braydon asked.

"There is something deep in you which I cannot reach," she answered, "and it is not fair. I give you my love, my heart, and my body – in fact everything that I own – and you give me very little in return."

Lord Braydon had not answered, he had merely kissed her.

For the moment she was content with his kisses, as she found him an extremely ardent lover.

However, when he left her she knew that she really possessed very little of him.

The rest was locked away, so to speak, in a secret place she could not reach.

"Promise that you will think of me when you are away," the same Beauty had whispered last night when he had said good-bye to her.

"I shall be counting the hours until I return," Lord Braydon replied.

She tried to take it as a compliment, knowing how much he resented having to leave London at this particular moment.

Yet she had the feeling that it was his own private life he resented leaving rather than the fact that he could not be with her.

Now, as the train started off Lord Braydon opened the newspaper which Watkins had put ready beside him.

He was not thinking of any woman he had left behind him, but of what a waste of time this whole journey was likely to be.

He had however taken the trouble yesterday afternoon to call at the Foreign Office to speak to the Foreign Secretary.

It would have been a mistake to have secrets from the Marquess of Salisbury.

When he told him what the Prince had asked him to do, the Marquess had said:

"I agree with you, Braydon, it will most probably be a waste of your time. All the same, you may possibly be successful where we have failed."

"You have been trying to find out about this gun?" Lord Braydon enquired.

The Marquess nodded.

"I have one of my most experienced and skilled men out there at the moment, but I have not had a word from him for the last month or perhaps it is longer. I fancy therefore he will return empty handed."

Lord Braydon's lips tightened and the Marquess went on:

"The Germans are fanatical in their fear of spies, and they guard their secrets very much better than we do, providing we have any!"

"You believe this gun really exists?" Lord Braydon enquired.

The Marquess shrugged his shoulders.

"Our most experienced Naval experts tell me that what we possess cannot be improved on. At the same time, the

Germans have a history of being very advanced in scientific experiments."

Lord Braydon was aware of this and as he rose to say goodbye he said:

"I shall try to be back in time to see my horses run at Newmarket. That is another reason why I resent leaving the country at this particular moment."

"I am sorry for you," the Marquess of Salisbury said with a smile, "at the same time, I am grateful to the Prince of Wales. If anyone can accomplish the impossible, it is you!"

"You flatter me," Lord Braydon replied, "but even that does not placate me at the moment!"

The Marquess laughed, but as Lord Braydon had left the Foreign Office he was frowning again.

Now as he opened the newspaper, he told himself that Prince of Wales or no Prince of Wales, he had no intention of wasting more time than necessary.

He had already decided on whom he would make a courtesy call when he reached Berlin.

He had invented a plausible pretext for visiting the German Capital.

He had also decided to visit a very beautiful Russian woman who he had known several years ago.

She was now married to one of the Kaiser's Secretaries of State.

If she was still as lovely as he remembered, and if there was still an invitation in her dark eyes, his journey might have some compensations.

After he had been travelling for nearly an hour Watkins appeared with his dinner.

There was a restaurant-car attached to the train.

Lord Braydon had no intention of struggling towards it, or eating what he considered inferior food.

His Chef on the yacht had therefore prepared a hamper of some of his favourite dishes.

Watkins brought in first a collapsible table from the compartment next door.

Having covered it with a clean cloth which bore Lord Braydon's monogram, he proceeded to serve an excellent four-course dinner.

There was pâté to start with, and soup that had been kept in a hay-basket.

Another hot dish had managed to travel the same way and still be at exactly the right temperature to be most palatable.

There was some excellent champagne to drink with the meal, followed by a special claret that had been kept for several years in his cellars until this year when it was perfect.

The meal ended with coffee from the silver coffee-pot.

Lord Braydon then accepted a small glass of Napoleon brandy which his grandfather had put down at the beginning of the last century.

He sat back comfortably, feeling more in accord with the world than he had previously.

Only when he felt that he might as well have an early night did he summon Watkins to make up his bed.

His valet fetched the steward in charge of the carriage.

While the two men were busy making the bed with Lord Braydon's own sheets and pillow-cases he went into the corridor.

He stood looking out into the darkness.

He was thinking again how much he would have preferred his destination to be Paris rather than Berlin.

Several people walked past him, but he did not look at them, staring deep in his thoughts, with unseeing eyes into the darkness.

Then he heard Watkins say:

"Everything's ready for you, M'Lord!"

With a sign of relief he went back into his compartment. His bed certainly looked inviting.

He was just about to start to undress when there was a knock on the door.

He wondered who it could be.

Before he could answer the knock came again as if whoever was outside was in a hurry.

"Come in!" Lord Braydon said sharply and the door opened.

To his surprise he saw a young woman standing there.

She was extremely pretty and he was aware that she had very large eyes in a small, rather thin face.

To his astonishment she came further into the compartment and shut the door behind her.

Lord Braydon was sitting on his bed and made no effort to rise.

Putting out her hand to hold onto the wall to steady herself she said:

"I . . I am sorry to . . disturb you . . please . . forgive me . . but I need your . . help."

"My help?" Lord Braydon questioned.

"I . . I know who you are . . and as you are English . . I . . thought perhaps you would be . . kind enough to help me."

"In what way?" Lord Braydon asked.

She glanced over her shoulder in a frightened way as if she was afraid of being overheard before she said:

"There is a man . . a German . . I sat opposite him in the restaurant-car and now . . he will not . . leave me alone."

Her voice trembled, and she went on as if with an effort:

"He has left me for the moment . . but he said he would come back . . and although I can . . lock my door . . I feel . . because he is so persistent . . that he may . . bribe the steward or . . find some way to . . open it."

Lord Braydon was a good judge of both men and women.

He had supposed when she first appeared that the girl wanted something from him personally.

Now he knew that she was speaking with absolute sincerity and she was in fact, very frightened.

"I . . I am sorry," she said again. "Very . . very sorry . . to trouble you . . but I do not know . . what to do."

She swayed a little from the movement of the train as she spoke and Lord Braydon suggested:

"Suppose you sit down and tell me who you are, and how you know who I am."

She obeyed him, sitting on the edge of his bed and turning her face towards him.

She had taken off her bonnet.

Her hair, neatly, if not particularly fashionably dressed, was fair with a touch of gold in it.

Her eyes were the grey-green of a mountain stream, but the pupils were dark with what Lord Braydon thought was fear.

"I know about you from the newspapers," the girl said in answer to his question, "and I also know that you own some magnificent horses."

"I like to think so," Lord Braydon said a little dryly. "And now tell me about yourself. Surely you are not travelling alone?"

She looked away from him as if she was embarrassed before she said:

"I know it is . . incorrect . . but my maid who would have come with me is getting old and was feeling ill at the last moment . . and there was nobody else I could . . ask at such . . short notice."

She stammered over the words, which Lord Braydon thought was surprising.

"Will you tell me your name?" he asked.

"Loelia . . Johnson."

There was a slight pause between the two words which told him she was not telling the truth.

"And you are going to Berlin?" he asked.

She nodded.

He was about to ask her if she had somebody to look after her when she arrived in that large, rather menacing City.

Then he told himself that it would be a great mistake to become involved with a young, unknown woman at this particular moment.

He therefore said:

"I can understand you are finding it difficult to look after yourself when you are unchaperoned. Have you any idea who the man is?"

"He told me his name was Baron Frederick von Houssen."

Lord Braydon memorised the name for future reference, then said:

"The only thing I can do for you, Miss Johnson, as we are fellow countrymen, is to ask my valet who is sleeping next door to exchange compartments with you."

Loelia's eyes lit up and she exclaimed:

"Will you . . really do . . that?"

"I am sure it will prevent the man from troubling you further."

"Thank you . . thank you!" she said. "I am more grateful than I can . . possibly say."

She drew in her breath and added:

"I never thought . . I never imagined I would have . . difficulties of this . . sort."

"I can only repeat," Lord Braydon said, "that it is always a mistake for any young lady such as yourself to travel alone."

"I . . I know that now," she said, "and I will try . . not to let it . . happen again."

Lord Braydon got to his feet.

"Stay here," he said, "while I speak to my valet."

He went from the compartment shutting the door behind him.

He called Watkins, who had not yet begun to undress, and told him what had happened.

"It don't surprise me, M'Lord," Watkins said, "foreigners is the same the world over! They thinks a young woman alone be easy prey."

"Well there is nothing we can do about it, Watkins," Lord Braydon said quickly, "but if you will exchange your compartment with Miss Johnson's I feel you will be able to deal with the amorous Baron when he returns."

Watkins grinned.

"Leave it to me, M'Lord!"

He went back to his compartment and begin to pick up his own belongings and the cases belonging to his Master.

Lord Braydon returned to where Miss Johnson was waiting for him.

She was still sitting where he had left her on the edge of the bed.

He had the strange feeling as he entered the compartment that she was praying.

Her hands were certainly clasped together and her eyes had been shut until he came close to her.

"It is all arranged," he said. "My valet will let me know as soon as he has taken his own luggage into your compartment and moved your things next door."

"You are . . so kind," Loelia said, "You are very . . clever . . as I thought you . . would be."

"Why should you think that?" Lord Braydon enquired.

She did not answer.

He thought that what she had said had come inadvertently to her lips and now she was regretting it.

"I asked you a question," he said after a moment.

"It is just . . that I have heard my father . . and other people . . speak about you and of how . . clever you are."

"Clever!" Lord Braydon repeated. "I cannot imagine why they should think so."

"Now you are being modest," Loelia replied.

Lord Braydon knew that socially amongst his own contemporaries he was not particularly noted for being clever.

But it was known to people like the Marquess of Salisbury, the Prince of Wales, and one or two other Ministers with whom he worked from time to time.

Socially he was noted for being an attractive, handsome man who was a good host.

It seemed strange that the girl sitting on his bed should refer to him like that, and after a moment he said:

"Did your father say in which way he thought I was clever?"

"No .. no .. of course not," Loelia said, "it was just an .. impression I got .. and of course .. I can see you have been very clever in .. arranging how to help me!"

Lord Braydon thought there was far more behind what she said than appeared on the surface.

Once again he told himself he must not get involved.

The best thing he could do would be not to probe too deeply, but keep their acquaintance as casual as possible.

He was helped at that moment by the door opening and Watkins coming in to say:

"I've got everything arranged, Miss, and all your things is next door."

"Thank you .. thank you very much."

Loelia rose to her feet as she spoke saying to Lord Braydon:

"Thank you once again, My Lord. I am very grateful .. more grateful than I can possibly .. say."

She went quickly from the compartment.

Lord Braydon could hear her soft voice talking to Watkins before the door was shut.

After that there was silence.

He locked his own door and started to undress.

As he did so, he thought it was a strange encounter.

He wondered once again why Miss 'Johnson' – he was sure that was not her name – talked about him as being 'clever'.

It would certainly not help his mission if the Germans thought he was clever.

He went over exactly in his mind the story he had prepared to explain why he should think it important to visit Berlin in the Middle of the London Season.

When he got into his bed, he found it difficult to sleep.

He lay thinking of the girl next door and what a mistake it was for anybody so young and attractive to travel alone.

She was obviously a Lady, and it seemed to him that even the stupidest parent or Guardian should not allow her to go careering across the Continent unattended.

Then he remembered how she had been reticent about her name.

He wondered if perhaps she was running away, and if so, from whom?

Then he told himself he was being ridiculous.

Whatever this young woman did or did not do, it would be a mistake for him to have anything to do with her.

He must certainly not waste time in thinking about her.

Instead he should be planning exactly how he should discover what the Prince of Wales and the Marquess of Salisbury wished to hear.

The train thundered on through the night.

Lying awake Lord Braydon began to think he was being haunted by the two grey-green eyes with an expression of fear in them.

. . . .

The train arrived in Berlin early in the morning.

Lord Braydon did not hurry to leave it, knowing it would wait in the station until all the passengers had alighted.

By the time he was dressed and Watkins had packed his sheets and pillow-cases, it was nearly nine o'clock.

He was not surprised when he came out of his own compartment to see that the door next to his was open.

Its occupant had gone.

At the station a carriage sent by the British Embassy was waiting to meet him.

As they drove away, Lord Braydon said to Watkins:

"Did the Baron who was pursuing Miss Johnson come to her compartment last night?"

Watkins grinned.

" 'E did, M'Lord, an' I gives him a piece o' m' mind! 'e started swearing at me, but 'ard words breaks no bones!"

Lord Braydon was amused.

As they drove on he wondered if Loelia had been met at the station and if she had managed to get away without encountering the Baron again.

The British Embassy had been notified of his arrival.

Lord Braydon however, had no intention of staying there as he had been invited to do.

He knew that would restrict his movements.

It would also be far more difficult to make the necessary enquiries without causing comment amongst the British Embassy staff.

He had therefore asked a friend who was working in the German Embassy in London for help.

He actually had an apartment in a building which was like an Hotel, except that Suites could be rented by the year.

The occupiers of them supplied their own furniture and if necessary, their own servants.

He had been only too pleased to put his apartment at Lord Braydon's disposal.

When he arrived he found it consisted of the whole of the Third Floor of the building.

It was exceedingly comfortable, furnished with every possible luxury, including a good supply of wine.

Even Watkins, who was always very critical of anywhere his Master stayed, said:

"This is much better, M'Lord, than some o' them sleazy hotels we've 'ad to put up wiv from time to time."

"I agree with you, Watkins, and I was rather afraid that if this turned out not to be comfortable we should have to suffer from the 'sleazy Hotels' as you call them."

He then started to send out letters which he had written before leaving England.

They were addressed to various people he wished to see while he was in Berlin.

He did not make the mistake of concentrating only on those who were concerned with the German Navy.

He made an exception however in the case of the

Captain of the '*Weissenburg*' whom he had met once at dinner when they were both in Cowes.

By the afternoon he had received two invitations to dinner that evening and several others for the following day.

He chose to dine with Baron Von Krozingen who he had met at Marlborough House.

He had said in his letter to him that he was bringing special messages from the Prince of Wales.

He knew this would attract an invitation.

It was written very effusively by the Baroness.

She stated that she and her husband were looking forward with the greatest pleasure to seeing him at eight o'clock.

As he dressed himself Lord Braydon was thinking how much he would have preferred to be in London.

He would be going to Marlborough House where he always enjoyed himself.

Alternatively having dinner with some beautiful lady whose husband was otherwise engaged.

Instead of which, from his experience of German society, he knew it would be an extremely formal evening.

The food would be heavy, the wines ordinary and the conversation stilted.

'Damn it all!' he ejaculated. 'Why did I consent to do this when it is quite certain that I shall discover nothing that is not known to our Navy already."

He knew the answer was quite simple: he could not refuse the Prince of Wales.

Not only because it was a Royal Command, but also because he was genuinely sorry for a man who had been so badly treated by his mother, the Queen.

The Prince had never been given a position of any authority in State Affairs.

He had been kept on 'the outside' until he had passed middle-age and he was still treated like an ignorant boy in his 'teens.

"I must find out something – anything – so long as he is the first to know," Lord Braydon told himself.

Then before he went downstairs he said to Watkins:

"It may be quite unnecessary, Watkins, but I should be glad if you would pick me up tonight at about 10.30 p.m. from Baron Von Krozingen's house."

He thought for a moment and went on,

"I may have a chance of going on elsewhere – I may not – but anyway, I would rather you were with me."

"That's wot I thought you'd say, M'Lord, an' I've already arranged for a carriage to be at our disposal."

"You have?" Lord Braydon asked in surprise.

"I knows Your Lordship's up to something, as usual, M'Lord," Watkins said, "an' naturally I wants to be in at the kill!"

It was an impertinence which Lord Braydon would not have endured from anyone except Watkins who had a very special place in his life.

As he turned towards the door he said:

"I very much doubt if there will be a 'kill' and it would certainly be a mistake for us to 'count our chickens'."

"I knows that, M'Lord," Watkins said, "but it's always a good idea to be prepared."

The way Watkins spoke made Lord Braydon laugh.

Downstairs he stepped into a comfortable carriage.

It was driven by a uniformed coachman supplied by the Baron to convey him to his house.

As the carriage moved off he told himself that he was very fortunate to have Watkins with him.

They had been in many tight spots in the past, but he doubted if they would find themselves in one on this trip.

CHAPTER TWO

The dinner-party was just as boring as Lord Braydon had anticipated.

The guests were middle-aged, pompous, and intent on impressing him with the superiority of everything that was German.

He had however deliberately chosen to dine with Baron von Krozingen.

This was because the Baron was closely connected with defence plans for the country.

He was quite certain that if anything secret or exceptional was being put in hand the Baron would be aware of it.

At the same time, he was a rather slow-brained man, very conscious of his own importance and determined that everybody else should be aware of it too.

He talked all through dinner about European politics.

He laid down the law in an aggressive manner which made Lord Braydon long to contradict him.

But he knew this would be a mistake, and instead he set himself out to be charming to his hostess and to everybody else in the party.

There was one thing that cheered him up through the long-drawn-out meal of very heavy over-cooked food.

It was the thought that tomorrow he would dine with the Princess who had answered his note immediately.

She had expressed her delight at his arrival in Berlin,

saying how much she was looking forward to seeing him again.

She had also added that she had unfortunately some friends dining with her tomorrow evening.

As they were elderly and liked to go to bed early, she was sure that he and she would be able to have a *tête-à-tête* after they had left.

With a faint smile Lord Braydon realised exactly what the *tête-à-tête* would entail.

He thought that, and that alone, would relieve his boredom at being in Berlin when he would so much rather have been in London.

The dinner dragged on.

The other guests ate what seemed an enormous amount of venison, dumplings, sauerkraut and apfelstrüdel.

They were all dishes which Lord Braydon detested and never ate if he could possibly avoid it.

He was very conscious that in order to keep his body athletic as he wished he must eat wisely and sparingly.

This was combined with his regular practice of boxing and fencing.

When he was in the country he rode for most of the day, and this had left him without an ounce of superfluous fat on his body.

Many women had told him that when he was unclothed he looked like a Greek god.

It was something he wished to believe himself.

He therefore took very little of each course and messed it about on his plate. In fact, he ate little more than a spoonful of each dish with which he was served.

The wine was slightly better than the food, but it could not be compared with his own cellar or what was provided for the guests at Marlborough House.

At last, when the ladies had left the Dining-Room he thought he would be able to escape.

However, the Baron after asking him to sit next to him said in a low voice:

"I have a treat for you after dinner, my dear boy!"

"A treat?" Lord Braydon questioned, raising his eyebrows.

The Baron gave him a knowing look that made him apprehensive.

He became even more so.

Having hastened the other guests on their way by making it clear that it was time for them to leave, the Baron dug his elbow into Lord Braydon's ribs and said:

"Now we can enjoy ourselves!"

Lord Braydon played with the idea of saying that he had another engagement, then thought it would be a mistake.

If he was to find out anything from the Baron, which he thought was unlikely, the only chance to do so was to play along with him.

He hoped that as he had drunk a great deal at dinner he might be indiscreet.

Lord Braydon said goodnight to the Baroness, who seemed not in the least surprised that her husband was going out without her.

Then they got into the Baron's large rather ostentatious carriage that was waiting for them outside.

As he stepped into it, Lord Braydon glanced down the road thinking that by this time Watkins would be waiting in case he was needed.

He knew that having seen him get into the Baron's carriage Watkins would follow.

He had found in the past that if he accepted a lift from his host for some riotous party it was often difficult to get away.

He had learnt it was essential therefore to have a conveyance of his own.

He knew too that Watkins, who spoke several European languages, was useful.

He would obtain information from the servants at any house at which he received hospitality.

Lord Braydon seated himself beside the Baron.

The footman put a light rug over their knees, and as he closed the door, the Baron said in his guttural voice:

"And now, my dear Braydon, I will be able to repay the hospitality you gave me when we were last in England."

Lord Braydon remembered that he had invited the Baron and Baroness to a large Reception he had given at his house in Park Lane.

He had included them among his guests simply because they were staying at the German Embassy.

It would have been insulting when they were with the Ambassador not to invite them.

"You are very kind," the Baron was saying, "and I was delighted on that auspicious occasion to meet the Prince of Wales."

"I am sure His Royal Highness enjoyed meeting you," Lord Braydon murmured diplomatically.

"It is a pity, a great pity," the Baron went on, "that he and our Emperor so often disagree with each other, and the disagreement usually appears to concern our ships!"

He laughed as if he had made a joke, then digging Lord Braydon once again in the ribs he said:

"Now I am going to show you some very pretty craft over which you and I will have no disagreements, and you are my guest."

Lord Braydon for the moment did not understand exactly what he meant.

Then he realised they had left the impressive Avenue in which he had been dining.

The carriage was in a quarter of the City which was notorious, and he understood.

The Baron was treating him to what was politely termed 'a House of Pleasure'.

Because he was exceedingly fastidious, Lord Braydon had always made it a rule, unlike his contemporaries, that he would never have a mistress whom he would have to pay in hard cash.

Nearly all the members of his Club patronised one of the well-known 'Houses' near St. James's.

Otherwise they had discreet little Villas in St. John's

Wood, where they kept an actress or a ballet-dancer under their protection.

Lord Braydon's *affaires de coeur* were carried out with the ladies he met at Marlborough House.

They were known as Professional Beauties, simply because postcard portraits of them were on sale in every stationers.

The curious stood on chairs in Hyde Park just to catch a glimpse of them as they passed.

They were all married, but their husbands, after five to ten years of 'matrimonial bliss' turned a 'blind eye' to any liaison.

Provided of course it was conducted with propriety and did not in any way impinge on their pride.

Somebody laughingly said that the 11th Commandment was: "Thou shalt not be found out!" although what it really meant was "There must be no scandal".

Lord Braydon had been aware from the Princess's letter that her Diplomat husband would be away when he dined with her tomorrow night.

So in London the husbands of the ladies who threw themselves into his arms were continually absent from home.

They were either at race-meetings or at appropriate times of the year shooting, fishing or hunting.

It was all conducted in a very civilised manner.

Therefore with horror Lord Braydon knew that, unless he was definitely to offend the Baron, he would find himself in a Brothel.

He thought of saying he felt ill, but knew it was hardly the sort of excuse his host would appreciate.

Then he told himself this was a challenge for his wits.

The Baron was still extolling the charms of the women he was going to meet when the horses came to a standstill outside a brightly lit doorway.

The red gas-lamp made it quite obvious what could be expected inside.

The Baron got out of the carriage and walked unsteadily up the steps.

Lord Braydon was aware that the Baron was far more drunk than he had thought when they left his house.

He knew this was the result of going out into the cool night air.

As they were welcomed effusively by the Madame in charge of the establishment he immediately began to pretend that he too had imbibed heartily.

The Baron was very much in his element.

He paid Madame, who, well over sixty was rouged, powdered and bewigged so that she looked like a stage parody, extravagant compliments.

They passed through the hall to enter a large room.

There was a comfortable sofa and a number of bottles of wine waiting for them.

At a quick glance Lord Braydon realised the hock should be drinkable, the claret was dubious, and the champagne had never seen a French vineyard.

He accepted a glass of hock while the Baron downed two glasses of claret in quick succession.

Then he started on the champagne.

While he was doing so the girls whom Madame had commanded to appear with a clap of her hands paraded in front of them.

They were mostly large, buxom, big-chested Germans.

There were two dark-haired girls who might have been French, and one who was obviously Chinese.

As they passed in front of the sofa, wearing only a wreath of roses or a large feather fan the Baron applauded.

He also called out to them by name.

Having finished the parade they mounted revolving silver balls, decorated with small pieces of looking-glass.

"What did I tell you Braydon?" the Baron shouted. "This is unique – something you will not see anywhere else in the world – and it is yours, all yours my dear chap, so make your choice."

He then explained to Madame as he had already done several times before that Lord Braydon was his guest, and that when the delights of the evening were over he was to be presented with the bill.

There was a pause while the Baron waited for Lord Braydon to reply.

He held out his glass for more although it was still half-full and said:

"You are the master *Mein Herr* and I am the pupil – I await your lead."

It sounded a complimentary remark and the Baron was delighted.

Struggling to his feet with some difficulty he stood in the centre of the revolving girls shouting compliments to each one of them.

Finally he threw his arms in a theatrical gesture and called two names.

The girls in question gave shrill cries of delight.

They jumped down from the revolving balls and ran to him, putting their fat arms around his neck and kissing his cheek.

They dragged him as if too impatient to wait to a door which opened at the end of the room and disappeared from sight.

"And now, *Mein Herr*, it's your turn," the Madame said in broken English.

Out of courtesy and also, Lord Braydon knew, because he liked to show how erudite he was, the Baron had spoken in English all evening.

The rest of the guests who had been at the party had followed suit.

Lord Braydon thought it was a good idea not to let any of them know how proficient he actually was in German.

Therefore, when Madame addressed him, he knew how he could excuse himself.

He had no intention of taking part in what to him was the very opposite of a 'treat'.

"I wanna girl wh'sh English," he replied slurring his words.

He knew as he spoke that he had found a way out of his difficulties.

He had been quite certain there was no English girl amongst those revolving on the silver balls.

He also thought it unlikely that there were many other women in the house at the moment.

That was not to say that he and the Baron were the only guests.

He suspected that as they had arrived rather late, business had already started long before they got there.

"I zink," the Madame said after a distinct pause, "you find Greta speak little English, also she verry experienced – make you very happy."

She began as she spoke to beckon one of the German girls with fair hair and a very plump body towards them.

Then when she stood in front of Lord Braydon he said:

"No! She'sh not English, an' if you can't give me an English girl I'll fin' one elsewhere."

He thought he had Madame defeated.

It would be an excuse for him to leave, leaving her to explain to the Baron later why he had done so.

Somewhat to his consternation she rose to her feet saying:

"Cum! Cum! *Mein Herr!*"

This was something Lord Braydon had not expected. He therefore deliberately made himself very unsteady on his feet.

He staggered after Madame out through a different door from the one used by the Baron.

She walked down a narrow passage and opened a door which Lord Braydon knew was near the Entrance Hall.

He saw, as he expected, a bedroom.

He guessed that it was used for those who found it difficult to walk far and certainly were incapable of climbing the stairs.

The room was decorated in the usual gaudy manner of such places.

A large bed was draped with curtains of pink satin and on the ceiling a large mirror.

The curtains over the window were the epitome of vulgarity.

Draped with bows and tassels they seemed more hideous than attractive.

There was a washhand-stand in one corner and in the other a cabinet.

Lord Braydon guessed it contained erotica of the sort which made him feel sick even to think about.

Otherwise there were touches of luxury that he was sure clients like the Baron expected. There was a large comfortable sofa for those who preferred it to the bed, and a thick carpet on the floor.

There were several other mirrors besides the one on the ceiling which reflected and re-reflected the room and its occupants.

There was also the inevitable table on which drinks could be served.

As soon as they entered the room a servant supplied them with a bottle of champagne.

Lord Braydon knew it would cost an exorbitant sum of money, whether it was opened or not.

To make sure the Madame understood what he had been saying, he repeated it.

He slurred his words even more than he had done before:

"I wan' an En'lish girl – no trisch – En'lish, like me!"

"You wait *Mein Herr*," the Madame answered quickly, "verry soon bring English girl."

She went from the room as she spoke, shutting the door behind her.

Lord Braydon sat down on the sofa.

He was thinking that if an English girl, which he doubted, was provided, he could say she was not to his taste.

He would give her enough money to assuage her hurt feelings.

It would certainly in the circumstances be easier to deal with somebody of his own nationality.

A German would be aggressive and consider herself insulted.

It was quite a long wait.

He decided with a smile that Madame would appear and say it was too difficult.

She would only apologise for failing him.

Then, just when he was thinking he could leave, saying there was no point in him staying any longer, the door opened.

Madame had come back.

She had her arm round the shoulders of a young girl who was wearing, Lord Braydon saw, a nightgown.

Over this was a negligée of bright pink muslin, trimmed with a coarse lace and numerous bows of velvet ribbon.

The girl's face as hidden, but he could see that she had long, fair hair.

As Madame moved with her slowly towards the bed Lord Braydon knew that the girl had been drugged.

Madame sat her down on the bed and shook her, digging her sharp fingers into her arms as she said:

"Do as the gentleman wants, or you'll be sorry!"

With that she released the girl and walking towards Lord Braydon said:

"She young an' shy! What better, *Mein Herr* than virgin, verry innocent – verry rare!"

She leered at him, then left the room quickly in case he should expostulate.

Only as the door shut did the girl on the bed raise her head and open her eyes.

As she did so Lord Braydon realised incredulously that it was Loelia.

She recognised him at the same time and exclaimed.

"You!"

Jumping up she ran towards him.

His quick brain made Lord Braydon realise first that something was very wrong.

Secondly he knew Loelia had pretended to be drugged.

She reached him and he realised she was about to fling herself against him, so he put his hand over her mouth to stop her from speaking.

At the same time he put his arm around her.

He turned his back so that anybody looking through the door would think that he was kissing her.

Then in a whisper that only she could hear he said:

"Do not speak! They will be listening and watching."

She understood and he felt her relax, but her eyes were pleading with him desperately.

When he took his hand from her mouth she did not speak.

"Get into the bed," he murmured against her ear.

Then in a loud voice, slurring his words as before, he said:

"You a ver' pretty li'll girl – jus' what I wash lookin' for, and' I can talk to you, an' undershstand what you're shaying – I find those Krauts unintelligible."

As Loelia went towards the bed he saw that she moved slowly. She would make anybody watching her think she was still under the influence of drugs.

Lord Braydon took off his evening-coat and hung it on the door handle. He had guessed from the size of the keyhole that they might be easily observed through it.

He then walked to the washing-stand and taking a towel hung it on a hook in the centre of the door.

He thought that there might be a concealed hole there through which they could be seen.

As he walked to the bed from where Loelia was watching him, with her eyes seeming to fill her pale face, he put his finger to his lips.

Then he looked behind the curtains and found, as he expected, a listening device.

It was not unlike an ear-trumpet, and was inserted through the wall.

Anybody listening in the adjacent room would be able to hear every word they said.

He took a handkerchief out of his pocket and stuffed it firmly into the tube.

He was certain it would now be completely ineffective.

Finally he sat down on the bed saying as he did so, in a low voice:

"What has happened? How did you get here?"

Loelia put out her hands to hold onto him as if she was afraid he might leave her and whispered:

"Save me . . please . . save me!"

"Tell me what has happened," Lord Braydon said. "I think it is very unlikely that we can be overheard, at the same time speak softly, and remember you are supposed to be amusing me."

The lights were seductively low.

He turned out a gaslamp over one of the looking-glasses to make it darker still.

Then he went round to the other side of the bed and lay down on it, saying as he did so:

"There might be a peep-hole in the ceiling, so lie down and put your face on the pillow facing me."

She obeyed him like a child.

When they were near enough for anyone watching to be satisfied they were doing what was expected Lord Braydon said:

"Now tell me what happened after you left the train."

"I . . I collected . . my luggage," Loelia said in a frightened little voice, "and walked out of the station. My Porter asked me: 'Are you alone, Miss?' and I said that I was and wanted a carriage to take me to a quiet hotel."

Loelia paused before she continued as she was trying to remember exactly what had happened.

"He kept looking at me and I had the idea it was because I was English . . even though I was . . speaking to him in . . German."

"Go on," Lord Braydon said.

"He walked past several carriages waiting for hire,

and went to one standing a little apart from the .. others and said:

"'This young lady's going your way, Ma'am, perhaps you'd give her a lift.'"

Loelia drew in her breath before she went on:

"I could not see very clearly inside the carriage, but a woman said to me in German:

"'Of course, I would be only too pleased. Jump in, my dear, and tell me where you want to go.'"

"So you did as she suggested!"

"I have been asking myself ever since .. how I could have been so .. foolish," Loelia replied, "but I had no .. idea that .. anything like .. that could .. happen!"

"I told you you should not be travelling alone."

"Yes .. I know .. and of course you were .. right."

"What happened after that?"

"The Lady, for that was what she seemed to me, asked where I was staying, and I asked her to recommend a respectable Hotel.

"'I have a better idea than that,' she said. 'I came to the station to meet my daughter, but I am afraid she is a careless young woman and once again must have missed her train.

"She smiled and went on:

"'That means she will not arrive until tomorrow. Her room is all ready for her, so I suggest you come with me and I shall be delighted for you to be my guest.'"

Loelia went on in an unhappy little voice:

"She seemed so kind .. and I was rather .. frightened of being alone .. in Berlin and not being .. certain of .. where I should go. So I thanked her .. and agreed."

"Surely you must have thought she looked strange?"

"She looked quite different from the way she does tonight," Loelia argued, "and when we drove out of the station I saw she was neatly dressed, and wore no make-up. It never struck me for a moment .. that she could .. look the way she .. does .. now . . . ."

Her voice faded away and Lord Braydon was aware that she was trembling.

Then as if she felt she must go on, Loelia said:

"When I came into .. this house I thought it seemed peculiar but I was hurried .. upstairs into quite a pleasant room, except that it was very over-decorated and the lady said to me,

"'Now take off your hat and coat and I am sure you would like something to drink. We will have luncheon early, but first I will bring you a cup of hot chocolate.'

"She did not wait for me to reply and as I was taking off my bonnet and tidying my hair she came back with the chocolate and said:

" 'Now drink it up, you will find it very pleasant, and I am ordering for you something special for luncheon.' "

"So you drank the chocolate," Lord Braydon remarked, knowing now what it contained.

"Yes .. I drank it because .. I was rather .. hungry then I knew .. nothing more.

"When I .. woke up," Loelia said in a voice of terror "It was late in the .. next morning and somebody had .. undressed me and .. put me to bed. For the .. first time I was afraid .. very afraid."

"You know exactly what sort of place you had been brought to?"

"No, of course not .. but I had heard of the .. white slave traffic and of how girls were .. picked up and .. carried off to .. foreign places .. and .. because it seemed so .. strange that she should have .. drugged the chocolate .. I was terrified."

There was a little pause, then Loelia went on, her voice shaking:

"She came into the room looking like you see her now. Then I .. guessed I was .. somewhere .. wicked .. horrible and .. evil."

"What did you do?" Lord Braydon asked.

"I told her I wanted to leave at once, but she laughed. She told me I was her prisoner and I would have to do as I was .. told .. otherwise I would be .. doped and .. beaten into .. submission."

Loelia put out her hand as she spoke to hold onto Lord Braydon.

"You will .. take me away? Promise you .. will take me .. away?"

"It is not going to be easy."

He thought as he spoke that if he made a scene Madame would undoubtedly protest violently.

It was the sort of story that might get into the newspapers.

It would also be extremely uncomfortable for him socially.

The Germans to whom he had written on his arrival were all aware that he was a close friend of the Prince of Wales.

To many of them he had said he had messages from the Prince which he wished to give them personally.

All this flashed through his mind, and as if she knew what he was thinking, Loelia said:

"Please .. please .. you cannot .. leave me here .. I have pretended all day to still be doped .. and I have eaten and drunk nothing .. in case they repeat what they .. gave me last night."

"That was intelligent of you," Lord Braydon said, "but you must be aware that they will try to stop you from leaving."

"H .. how can I .. stay," she asked as a child might have done, "unless I .. kill myself?"

Instinctively Lord Braydon's fingers tightened on hers and he said:

"I will save you somehow, although, God knows, it is going to be difficult."

"But you .. will save me? I know it is a .. great deal .. to .. ask .. but you cannot .. leave me .. here in this .. horrible place."

She gave a little sob as she said:

"I .. had no .. idea there were .. places like this .. and I did not realise .. that gentlemen like you .. would come to them."

"I came here tonight because it would have been very

difficult for me to refuse to accompany my host," Lord Braydon explained. "And I asked for an English girl, being sure they would not be able to provide one."

He paused and went on quietly.

"That would give me a good excuse for leaving without having to participate in the 'amusements' which are provided."

"But you . . cannot leave me . . please . . please . . you cannot leave me."

"I realise that," Lord Braydon agreed. "But now before we go any further, you must tell me why you are in Berlin, and also your real name."

"Then you realise . . I was . . lying when I said it was Johnson?"

"You are not a very good liar," he said, "and I still do not understand why you are travelling alone when you are obviously very inexperienced and far too pretty, as I said before, not to be chaperoned."

Loelia looked at him.

"I . . I came to . . Berlin to f . . find my . . f . . father."

"And you do not know where he is?"

"I have . . no idea . . but I think the . . Germans are holding him prisoner."

Lord Braydon stiffened.

"Why should they have done that?"

She did not answer him for a moment and he said:

"You cannot expect me, Loelia, to help you if you are not frank with me. Tell me the Truth – the whole Truth – otherwise, I shall be obliged to leave you to look after yourself!"

She gave a cry of horror.

Then she instinctively shut her lips as if afraid she might be overheard.

"Trust me," Lord Braydon said very quietly.

"I ought not to talk . . of things which concern only Papa . . but if I tell you the truth . . would you be very careful not to hurt him?"

She spoke with a depth of sincerity which told Lord

Braydon her father was very important to her, and he replied:

"I am concerned at this moment primarily with getting you out of this mess into which you have inadvertently fallen. At the same time I have to make sure that you are not tricking me in some way."

He spoke deliberately.

He knew by the expression in her eyes how shocked she was that he should think that was what she might be doing.

"I swear to you .. before God," she said, "and by everything I hold Holy .. that I am not concerned in .. anything that involved you .. but only in trying to help my father .. who I know is .. in trouble."

"Did he tell you so?"

"No .. no .. but I can .. feel it."

"How?"

"You will not .. believe me if I .. tell you."

"I will try to do so."

"Very well .. I am so close to Papa .. and have been with him all the time ever since .. Mama died .. that I can feel things about him when he is not with me that .. other people would not be .. able to do."

She spoke hesitatingly as if she knew that Lord Braydon would not believe her.

It was difficult to put what she meant into words.

However, he helped her by asking:

"Are you telling me that you have psychic or supernatural perceptions or feelings about him?"

"Papa believes it is quite simply the Power of Thought," Loelia replied.

"I have of course heard of that," Lord Braydon answered, "but mostly in connection with the people of India and other parts of the Orient. I did not think it was practised in England."

"Papa said the same thing, but just as I can read his thoughts and he can read mine, I know what is happening to him when he is not with me and .. I am aware now that he is being held a prisoner!"

"How can you possibly know that?" Lord Braydon asked.

She gave a helpless little gesture with the hand which had been holding his and said:

"I knew you would not . . believe me."

"I am trying to do so, but you have not yet told me your father's name."

"It is Standish."

Lord Braydon stared at her, then he said:

"Are you telling me that your father is Thurston Standish?"

"You know him? You know Papa . .? I can hardly . . believe it!"

The name of Thurston Standish meant a great deal to people like Lord Braydon who were sometimes entrusted by the Foreign Office, as he had been, with special missions to other countries.

Thurston Standish was one of those prodigies who turn up occasionally in various parts of the world.

A man who finds it easy to speak any language, however difficult it might seem to other people.

He was an acknowledged expert on everything that concerned the Orient. And, because it interested him, he was a leading authority on the weapons of war.

It was a strange combination, but to Lord Braydon his name had been whispered on several occasions with awe and admiration.

With it, was the information that Thurston Standish knew more about the scientific experiments taking place in Russia and in certain other parts of the world than any other man alive.

He was a man Lord Braydon had always longed to meet.

It therefore seemed extraordinary, so extraordinary that he could not believe that he was not dreaming, that he should now be in contact with Thurston Standish's daughter.

Also that she should be in Berlin looking for her father.

Before he spoke it flashed through his mind that Thurston Standish might be the man of whom the Marquess of Salisbury had spoken.

The man he had sent to Berlin to try to find out about the new gun, but for over a month had made no report.

It was just the sort of assignment Lord Braydon thought that Thurston Standish would find fascinating.

If he was in danger, as his daughter thought, whatever else he did he must try to rescue him.

"I know your father only by reputation, and I have never met him,' he said, in answer to Loelia's question, "but I am aware of how brilliant he is and how he is trusted and admired by people whom we had best not mention here."

Loelia gave a little shiver.

She looked around the room, almost as if she thought somebody might be lurking in the shadows.

Then she said:

"It was foolish . . of me to come . . but I knew that Papa was in trouble . . and I thought he might be able to tell me how I could help him if I were . . nearer to him that I was in England."

"You knew he was in Berlin?"

"Yes, he told me he was coming here . . and he wrote to me from where he was staying every week until . . suddenly the letters stopped."

"It was then you think he was taken prisoner?"

Loelia gave him a strange glance from her large eyes before she said:

"I think Papa is trying to tell me that the Germans want to extract some information from him, and that is why they are holding him somewhere."

Lord Braydon thought this was very likely.

If the Germans could get their hands on a man like Thurston Standish they would try to persuade him to talk.

If they did, they could learn from him any secrets the

British Admiralty might have.

Also they could estimate whether their own new weapon was as superior as they believed it to be.

Lord Braydon knew now that there was no question of his not doing his best to rescue Loelia.

After that his next task would be to see what he could do about her father.

For a moment he felt helpless.

Then as always when he was in difficulty or danger, he knew there was a power which he could call on.

It had never failed him in the past.

Once again Loelia was reading his thoughts.

"If you can help me," she said, "then we can save Papa together, and I feel sure God must have sent you just at the . . right moment to do . . that."

The way she spoke was very moving and Lord Braydon said:

"We will have to be clever, very clever indeed, to get you out of this filthy place, and to make certain that no one makes a great fuss about it."

His brain was working like a well-oiled machine that started by moving slowly, then revolved more and more quickly.

He reckoned that he and Loelia had by now been together for nearly half-an-hour.

He had no wish to encounter the Baron until he had got her away.

Instinctively, almost as if the words were dictated to him, he told her what she had to do.

Because she was her father's daughter he realised she was used to obeying instructions to the letter.

She did not argue, she merely nodded.

Lord Braydon got off the bed.

Picking up the bottle of champagne, he poured most of it away in a corner of the room where it would not be discovered until after he had left.

Then he went behind the bed and retrieved his handkerchief from the tube and put it back into his pocket.

In his drunken voice he had used before he said loudly:

"You're very goo' girl – very goo' indeed! An' I shall return tomorrow!"

As he spoke he walked across the room, lifted his coat from the door-knob and put it on.

At the same time he untied his tie and several buttons of his waistcoat so that he looked dishevelled.

He ran his fingers through his hair, and beckoned to Loelia.

As she slipped out of bed, he put his arm around her shoulders and opened the door.

As he expected, as soon as they stepped out and moved into the hall the Madame was beside them.

"You had good time?" she asked gutterally. "Loelia good girl – do what you want?"

"Very good girl!" Lord Braydon replied with a hiccup, "very good – indeed! I will come back tomorrow night – an' you keep her for me."

"*Ja, ja, Mein Herr,* Loelia be kept for you."

Walking with difficulty and as if he might fall down at any moment, Lord Braydon leaned heavily on Loelia.

He walked with his arm around her to the front-door.

A servant opened it, then ran down two steps to where outside a carriage was waiting.

With relief Lord Braydon saw Watkins sitting on the box.

"Your carriage here, *Mein Herr?*" Madame said. "Say goodnight to Loelia. Verry pleased you like her."

"I think she'sh shplendid!" Lord Braydon said.

He saw several of the girls peeping at him through the door and called out:

"You all shplendid! Shplendid place, good girls, good Madame! I thank you!"

As he spoke he put his hand in his pocket.

Drawing out a number of notes and coins he flung them into the hall.

With shrieks of delight the girls fell on them.

In the rush to pick them up Madame bent forward towards a gold coin, that had fallen against her foot.

Lord Braydon flung several more coins towards the porter standing at the carriage-door who tried to snatch them.

As he did so he released Loelia and gave her a push.

Quick as lightning, she rushed down the steps, across the pavement, and flung herself into the carriage.

With the swiftness of an athlete who was certainly not intoxicated, Lord Braydon followed her.

The horses started off, and Watkins who had come down from the box sprang into the carriage pulling the door to.

The horses gathered speed, and Loelia gave a little cry and flung herself against Lord Braydon.

"We have done it! We have done it!" She cried. "I never believed it . . I never thought it was possible . . but we have . . done it!"

As she spoke she hid her face against his shoulder and he knew she was crying.

"It is alright," he said gently. "You have been very brave."

He looked across the carriage at Watkins who was sitting on the seat with his back to the horses.

The candle-lantern above him showed only too clearly the grin on his face.

"Now Watkins," Lord Braydon said, "we have to get Miss Loelia into the apartment without anybody thinking it is strange, but she is somewhat unclad."

"You've left your cape behind, M'Lord?"

"I am aware of that," Lord Braydon answered, "and my hat which was balanced rather precariously on my head, fell off as I was running down the steps."

As he had swayed drunkenly towards the front-door Madame had put his hat on the back of his head.

She had been holding his cloak over her arm, with the intention of giving it to him when he released Loelia.

"May I make a suggestion, M'Lord?" Watkins asked.

"Yes, of course," Lord Braydon agreed.

"I thinks, M'Lord, I'd best go up on the box beside the coachman. It's unlikely Your Lordship's been followed but one never knows."

Lord Braydon nodded.

When Watkins tapped on the glass window behind the coachman's seat, the horses were drawn to a standstill.

He jumped out to scramble up onto the box, and once again they set off at a sharp pace.

Loelia still had her face hidden against Lord Braydon's shoulder.

He was aware that she was fighting to control her tears.

"I will take care of you," he said, "but as there may be a hue and cry for you tomorrow, I think it would be a mistake to use your father's name in case you are in any way connected with him."

She raised her head to look at him.

He could see the tears glistening on her cheeks.

In a soft voice with a sincerity that seemed to come from her very heart:

"How can I . . ever thank . . you? How can I . . tell you how . . wonderful it was of . . you to take me . . away."

"You will be able to thank me when we and your father are out of danger," Lord Braydon said.

"I shall always think that if you had not come tonight there might have been . . somebody very different . . and I could not . . continue being . . doped and . . eating nothing."

"No, of course not. But try not to think about it. For the moment we have won the first battle, but doubtless there will be a number of others in which we have to be equally successful."

"I am praying . . praying very hard . . that we . . shall be," Loelia said.

"Now, as Watkins suggested," Lord Braydon said, "we

had better do something to cover you. I suggest you put this rug over your head."

He unfolded it, then added.

"It is large enough to cover you, and if you tuck your feet back, no one will know how you are dressed."

She gave him a little look which told her she thought he was being very clever.

The rug was made of light cashmere and he pulled it round her so that it covered her completely.

He thought there would not be too many servants about at this hour of the night.

At the same time, he did not wish to start people talking.

He wanted to give himself time to think.

He had to find a story which would convince the Baron, who would undoubtedly be involved in all this, that he had done what was right.

The carriage came to a standstill and Watkins opened the door.

Lord Braydon got out and picking Loelia up in his arms carried her across the pavement to the lighted door.

There were two porters on duty.

Although they looked somewhat curiously at what Lord Braydon was carrying in his arms, they asked no questions.

He walked to the lift and then went up to the Third Floor. Watkins accompanied them.

Once they were inside the apartment Lord Braydon put Loelia down on the ground.

Although she pushed the rug off her head, she held it around her and he knew she was shy.

"There's a bedroom along 'ere, Miss," Watkins said helpfully, taking control of the situation. "I knows as 'ow the bed's made up as I looked in all th' rooms as soon as we arrived."

He led the way and Loelia and Lord Braydon followed him.

It was a very pleasant room on the other side of the Sitting-Room.

It was obviously used by the owner of the apartment as a guest-room.

"Thank you very much," Loelia said to Watkins.

"And now, as Miss Loelia has had nothing to eat all day," Lord Braydon said, "I suggest you find her something substantial before she goes to sleep."

"Leave it t'me, M'Lord."

"I shall be . . all right," Loelia replied. "I do not want to be any . . trouble!"

Lord Braydon laughed.

"You have been a great deal of trouble already, and I think you will be a great deal more in the future. So the trouble you are putting Watkins to is a very minor affair."

Loelia sat down on the bed. Then she said:

"Now that I am . . safe, all I can really think about is Papa . . and what we . . can do . . about him."

"Are you absolutely convinced that he is being held captive?" Lord Braydon asked. "You realise it is not a question I can go about asking everybody to substantiate."

"I know he is!" Loelia asserted. "I can actually see because he is sending it to me in my thoughts, the room he is in."

Lord Braydon thought privately that he did not believe a word of this, but he was prepared to listen and she went on;

"It is in the basement of a big house, and in the room there is a table and a lot paper on which he is supposed to write or draw what the Germans wish to . . know."

"How can you possibly know that?" Lord Braydon asked.

She made a helpless little gesture with her hand and replied:

"If you do not . . believe me . . I'm afraid I have nothing . . more tangible by which I can . . convince you."

"I want to believe you, I really do, but you are making it very hard for me."

Loelia laughed and it was a very happy sound.

"That is what Mama used to say when I gave her messages from Papa which, for some reason which I never understand . . she could not receive herself."

"The story is absolutely extraordinary! I want to think it over carefully and try to work out how we can use these thought-powers of yours to help your father."

"If you will do that . . then I am quite certain we shall . . find him," Loelia said, "but I shall also be praying . . praying very . . hard that we shall be . . successful."

"Now that I *am* prepared to believe in!" Lord Braydon said quietly.

CHAPTER THREE

Loelia awoke and for a moment could not remember where she was.

Then as the horror of the night came flooding back to her she got out of bed to draw back the curtains.

The sun was shining on the grey houses which were somehow menacing.

She felt a little tremor run through her as she thought of her father.

Then she remembered her own plight.

Although she was safe for the moment, she had no clothes except the nightgown she had on.

She heard a knock on the door and hastily ran back to the bed.

Getting into it she pulled the sheet up high over her breasts.

Then in a nervous voice she called out:

"Come in!"

The door opened and Watkins peeped round it to say:

"Mornin', Miss! I 'ears you pullin' back the curtains and knew you was awake. Are you ready for some breakfast?"

Loelia smiled at him.

"I am indeed!" she replied. "And actually very hungry!"

Watkins had given her something to eat before she went to sleep last night.

She had, however, been without food all day in her fear of being drugged and was in fact ready now to eat anything.

It was only minutes before Watkins came in with a tray.

There were eggs and bacon, hot toast and a pot of coffee.

"The Master says, Miss," Watkins announced as he put down the tray, "that he'd like you to dress as soon as is convenient."

"Dress?" Loelia exclaimed. "In what?"

Watkins grinned.

"I only 'opes I've chosen what you likes," he said modestly.

"You have been shopping for me!" Loelia exclaimed incredulously.

"I could only guess at your size, Miss," Watkins replied, "but I've done me best."

He went from the room as he spoke.

Loelia, eating her breakfast with relish, thought that everything that was happening to her was quite astonishing.

She was also inexpressibly grateful to Lord Braydon.

She did not like to think of what would have happened if he had not come to that terrible place last night.

She had only a vague idea of what actually took place there, but she was aware of how terrifying and degrading it could be.

She was finishing her second cup of coffee when Watkins came back.

He was carrying the clothes he had bought for her.

She was surprised to see that they were simple and in good taste.

They were the sort of dresses that would be worn by a very young girl.

"The Master says, Miss," Watkins told her, "that he 'opes you'll be able to choose somethin' better for yourself, but in the meantime these'll 'ave to make do."

"They look very smart!" Loelia said quickly. "It is very

kind of his Lordship to be so considerate and very clever of you to buy clothes for somebody you have hardly seen."

"I only 'opes they fits," Watkins said. "And now, Miss, I'll get your bath ready."

Loelia knew it was unusual for there to be a bath in an apartment.

Although she knew there were bathrooms in some of the houses in England, they were never used by ladies.

They always bathed in their own bedrooms.

She did not say anything however when a little later Watkins brought her a large Turkish towel to cover her nightgown.

He then let her across the passage to where there was a very up-to-date bathroom with hot and cold running water laid on.

It was a luxury she had never thought of enjoying.

As she lay back in the warm water she felt it washed away some of the terror she had experienced yesterday. Also the degradation of the things Madame had said to her.

Then she told herself sensibly that what she had to think of now was her father.

He was still in her thoughts when she was dressed and Watkins told her that Lord Braydon was waiting to see her in the Sitting-Room.

It was the next room to hers and as she entered he rose from the desk at which he was sitting in the window.

She thought how strong he looked and how safe and secure.

She thought if only she could stay with him nothing terrible would happen to her again.

Impulsively she ran across the room and when she was beside him she said:

"Thank you . . thank you! I do not know . . how to put into . . words how . . grateful I am."

"We have other things to talk about at the moment," Lord Braydon said firmly.

She looked up at him wide-eyed and he went on:

"I think you are intelligent enough to realise that there may be serious repercussions over our behaviour last night. There is a possibility that the Germans may say that I have abducted you and call it a criminal offence."

Loelia gave a cry of horror.

"You are .. not trying to say .. I may have to .. go back?"

"No, of course not," Lord Braydon said quickly, "but I warn you that we can expect a visit from Baron von Krozingen who was my host last night, and we must have our story ready."

Loelia clasped her hands together.

"You will not mention Papa, or tell him who I really am?"

"I am not a fool," Lord Braydon replied, "and I imagine since you told me on the train that your name was Johnson, that you have a passport made out in that name?"

Loelia nodded.

"It belongs to Papa's secretary. I took it from her desk without .. telling her where I was .. going."

"That was intelligent of you," Lord Braydon approved. "We do not want the Germans to know that Thurston Standish's daughter is in Berlin."

He paused for a moment before he said as if he was considering his words:

"I have been thinking out what is the best thing to say, and to save time, as I have a feeling the Baron may arrive at any moment, I am going to suggest that you and Watkins both listen carefully to what I say to him."

"How can we do that?" Loelia asked.

"My bedroom door opens into this room," Lord Braydon explained, "and Watkins has already oiled the lock."

As he spoke the door into the passage opened and Watkins said in a warning voice:

"There's someone at the door, M'Lord!"

Without replying Lord Braydon walked quickly across the room and opened a second door by a bookcase.

Knowing exactly what she must do, Loelia hurriedly went into the bedroom and closed the door behind her.

She stood near the door.

Because she realised how quiet she must be she took off the slippers which Watkins had provided for her.

They were comfortable, if a little large.

She put them down on the carpet, then stood as near to the door as possible.

She could hear Watkins announce in a loud voice:

"The Baron von Krozingen to see you, M'Lord!"

Lord Braydon rose from the desk which gave the impression that he had been writing.

Holding out his hand he said in a tone of apparent surprise:

"My dear Baron, how kind of you to call so early in the morning!"

The Baron took his hand.

There was, however, an expression in his eyes which Lord Braydon was aware forecast trouble.

"It may be early," he went on, "but I think we might indulge ourselves by drinking a glass of the very excellent French champagne that my host has put at my disposal."

The Baron replied in a somewhat lofty manner:

"That certainly sounds a good idea!"

As he spoke, Watkins walked into the room.

He was carrying a tray on which reposed a bottle of Pol Roger and two glasses.

The bottle was open, and Lord Braydon poured out a glass for the Baron and one for himself.

Then they sat down in two comfortable armchairs and the Baron, having drunk half a glass, said:

"I am afraid, My Lord, I must take you to task for your behaviour last night!"

"That is certainly something I must explain," Lord Braydon replied.

As he spoke he put down his glass of champagne.

Then there was a pause as he stared across the room as if he was considering what he should say.

"You must be aware," the Baron interposed, "that it is unforgivable for anyone to take away from a – 'House of Pleasure' one of its inmates. After you had left, Madame was in a frenzied state and threatening to send for the Police."

"I was afraid that might happen," Lord Braydon said, "and that is why, while I owe you an apology and of course an explanation, I intend to trust you with some information which must in fact, be completely and absolutely confidential."

"I doubt if that could be possible," the Baron said aggressively.

"I think when you hear what I have to say, you, as a man of the world and of course a very distinguished Statesman, will understand that what I confide to you must never be divulged to anybody else."

The Baron's interest was obviously now aroused.

Lord Braydon rose to fill his glass of champagne before he said:

"Before I left England, I was told that Her Majesty the Queen and my grandmother the Dowager Duchess of Exmouth were giving their approval to a marriage between my Ward, who was living with my grandmother, and one of her Majesty's most favoured Lords-in-Waiting."

The Baron was now staring at him in undisguised astonishment.

Lord Braydon knew that he was wondering how this could possibly have any bearing on what had occurred last night.

"Unfortunately," Lord Braydon continued, "the Lord-in-Waiting, who I think should be nameless, is very much older than my Ward.

"Although he is a distinguished man with many years of service to the Crown, he is not exactly the romantic hero to capture the fancy of a very young girl."

He drank a little champagne before he continued:

"Like many of the young people of today, my Ward has independent and what older people think of as 'revolutionary' ideas.

"The most important reason why she objects to marrying him is, she says, because she wants to be in love with the man she marries."

The Baron nodded as if he understood and Lord Braydon went on:

"She therefore violently opposed the idea of such a marriage and when my grandmother told her there was no question of her not accepting Her Majesty's decision in the matter, she decided to enlist my sympathy."

There was a faint expression in the Baron's somewhat protruding eyes.

It told Lord Braydon he was beginning to understand where this tale was leading.

"Finding that I had already left for Berlin," Lord Braydon continued, "the foolish girl rushed to the station to take a train to Dover, and the cross-Channel Steamer to Antwerp.

"As it happened I had crossed the Channel to Antwerp in my yacht."

He paused and continued.

"By sheer chance my ward boarded the same train that I was on, but as it was already dark, she was not aware that I was within reach."

Lord Braydon again filled up the Baron's glass before he went on:

"When my Ward arrived in Berlin, having no idea that I was on the same train, she collected her luggage and asked the porter to recommend a quiet Hotel.

"By this time, she had had time to think over her impulsive action, and was sure I would be extremely annoyed with her not only for trying to follow me, but also for travelling along unaccompanied by a maid."

"Something any young lady should know is unacceptable!" the Baron murmured.

Lord Braydon ignored the remark and went on:

"She thought I would be staying at the British Embassy, and was afraid that the Ambassador would insist and so would I, that she returned to London immediately.

"She therefore decided to wait outside the Embassy, waylay me alone and try to persuade me to help her, or rather to ask Her Majesty to change her mind."

"A very difficult task," the Baron commented.

"An impossible one!" Lord Braydon agreed. "But I have not yet finished my story."

"I can guess what happened," the Baron growled.

"Madame offered her a lift, and you and I, as men of the world, can guess what happened next."

Lord Braydon rose to his feet to stand in front of the empty fireplace before he continued:

"I cannot contemplate what would have happened to this poor, misguided child, for she is little more, if she had not by some extraordinary quirk of fate been brought to me last night, rather than to a perfect stranger!"

Lord Braydon's voice changed as he said in a very different tone:

"You can however, my dear Baron, realise the horrifying implications of this story should it ever reach the ears of the Press."

He made a gesture with his hands.

"Not only would my Ward's reputation be torn into shreds, but you and I, both men of importance in our own lands, would be pilloried for indulging in the lusts of the flesh."

Lord Braydon's voice seemed to ring out as he said:

"We both know how certain newspapers in my country and here in yours, which are only too willing to discredit both the Monarchy and the establishment, would publicise such an episode."

"*Ja, ja*, I understand," the Baron said hastily, "as you say, My Lord, it would be utterly disastrous if it were known to the public."

"I am thinking more about you than of myself," Lord

Braydon said. "After all, I have a position at Court and I am honoured to have the Prince of Wales as my friend."

He stared at the Baron and went on:

"You are particularly vulnerable in that you are known to have a position of trust with regard to Naval Administration."

He lowered his voice before he said:

"Perhaps I should not tell you this, but in fact, I heard a rumour before I left England that the Russians suspect you of having a new secret weapon which they would like to add to their own Armoury and are therefore obviously spying on you."

"Spying on me – the Russians!" the Baron exclaimed in horror.

"It may of course be untrue," Lord Braydon said, "but they believe you have a new kind of mine or gun, I have no idea which, and of course they covet it for their own Navy.

"Then they are mistaken, utterly mistaken!" the Baron said sharply. "The new gun has nothing to do with me – nothing!"

"The Russians invariably get everything wrong," Lord Braydon said politely, having learned what he wished to know.

"But what is important," he went on, "is that I must ask you, my dear Baron, to make sure, from your point of view as well as my own, that what happened last night is talked about as little as possible. I am sure I can leave that in your capable hands."

The Baron nodded.

"I will see that Madame does not talk," he agreed, "although it may be somewhat expensive."

He looked expectantly at Lord Braydon who replied:

"I anticipated that, and here is a cheque which I think will cover any expenses you are obliged to incur in the matter."

He took a cheque from his desk and put it into the Baron's hands. The Baron looked at it and said:

"Generous, very generous! I can promise you, My Lord, there will be no more difficulties."

"What I want is to make sure that nobody knows my Ward is staying here with me in Berlin," Lord Braydon said, "and I must take her back to England as quickly as possible."

"Very wise," the Baron agreed.

He looked at Lord Braydon and added:

"You must forgive me, but I am still curious as to why you came to Berlin in the first place."

Lord Braydon smiled.

"I rather anticipated you might asked me that, and of course again I must ask you to keep anything I tell you confidential."

"Of course, of course," the Baron agreed.

"It is quite a simple matter for us at any rate," Lord Braydon said, "but of great import to the Prince of Wales."

The Baron looked at him enquiringly but he did not speak, and Lord Braydon said:

"You are well aware, I am quite certain, of the trouble there was last year at Cowes, when the Kaiser withdrew his racing yacht '*Meteor I*' from the race for the Queen's Cup on the grounds that the handicap was unfair to him."

"I remember his saying that," the Baron replied.

"The Prince of Wales learnt that before leaving Cowes the Kaiser had asked George Lennox Watson, the designer of the '*Britannia*' to build him a yacht which would be even faster than '*Meteor I*'."

Again the Baron nodded and Lord Braydon knew his knowledge of Naval affairs made him well aware of all this.

"What the Prince of Wales has asked me to find out on this trip is whether the yacht is actually being built, and if the Kaiser intends to race it at Cowes next year."

The Baron laughed.

"So that is your mission, My Lord."

"He wanted me to find out without people of importance like yourself being aware of my curiosity," Lord Braydon replied.

Now the Baron gave a loud laugh before he said:

"I can give you the answer quite truthfully, and it is that His Majesty will undoubtedly race *'Meteor II'* at Cowes, but I doubt if it will be ready for at least two years."

Lord Braydon gave a sigh of relief.

"Then that saves me an enormous amount of trouble, Baron, and I can only express once again my deepest regrets for having involved you last night in a very awkward situation. But there was nothing I could do to warn you what would happen after I left."

"*Nein, nein*, I understand," the Baron said. "Nothing else was possible in the circumstances."

"I knew you would understand," Lord Braydon said warmly. "May I also thank you now for a delightful dinner-party, and I shall look forward when next you and your charming wife come to England to returning your hospitality by giving a party for you at Bray House."

"We shall look forward to it," the Baron said.

He put down his glass reluctantly before he rose to his feet.

"Is there anything else I can do for you?" he enquired.

"Not at the moment," Lord Braydon answered, "but thank you for the suggestion, and thank you too for saving me a great deal of trouble over *'Meteor II'*."

The Baron chuckled as he said with satisfaction:

"I do not think the Prince of Wales's *'Britannia"* will have a dog's chance against her!"

Lord Braydon moved towards the door, saying just before he reached it:

"Now take care of yourself, my dear Baron, for I know how indispensible you are to the Kaiser and I do not trust the Russians."

"I cannot think why they should suppose that I have anything to do with the new invention on which the

Kaiser is so intent," the Baron said angrily. "That is Edersnier's job, and I only hope he will not make a mess of it."

Then as he felt he had been indiscreet he said:

"Nothing we have said to each other will of course go further than these four walls?"

It was a question and Lord Braydon said hastily:

"I am relying entirely on you, Baron, to protect my Ward's name and conceal the fact that Her Majesty is indirectly involved in this mess."

"You can leave it to me," the Baron said.

The two men passed through the doorway into the passage.

Lord Braydon ushered his guest into the lift, took him down to the Ground Floor and saw him into his carriage which was waiting outside.

When he returned he found Loelia waiting for him with her eyes shining.

As he came into the Sitting-Room she ran towards him saying excitedly:

"You are . . brilliant! You are . . so clever! I only wish Papa could have heard you getting the . . name out of him of the man who must be holding Papa a . . prisoner."

"How can you be sure of that?" Lord Braydon asked quietly.

There was a little silence, then Loelia said:

"While he was speaking of the gun, I concentrated on the Baron's thoughts, and I think I know what this man Edersnier looks like."

"You do?" Lord Braydon exclaimed. "Then tell me!"

"He is older than the Baron," Loelia said in a low voice, "and he had a moustache that turns up at the corners like the one worn by the Kaiser and it is white like his hair."

Lord Braydon stared at her before he asked:

"How can you possibly know anything like that?"

"I know you do not believe me, and you think I am talking nonsense," Loelia said, "but Papa taught me how to read people's thoughts in the way he does, and when you spoke of the gun, the Baron was thinking of the man concerned with it, and that is what he looked like."

"If it is true, it is certainly helpful," Lord Braydon said.

He walked across the room and pushed open the door of his bedroom.

It was ajar as he expected it to be.

He knew that Watkins would have opened it just a crack so that he and Loelia could hear what was being said.

Watkins was tidying his clothes in the wardrobe and Lord Braydon said to him:

"Where do you think I can find a picture of the man the Baron mentioned?"

"That won't be difficult, M'Lord," Watkins replied. "Everybody knows them Germans is keen on 'avin' their photos taken and the shops is full of 'em."

"Then go and see what you can find," Lord Braydon said.

"Leave it ter me, M'Lord," Watkins replied. "I'll also buy something for Miss Loelia's lunch if she's to eat here."

"She will eat here," Lord Braydon said firmly, "and as you are aware, Watkins, I have a luncheon appointment."

Loelia made a little murmur of protest.

"Must you go?" she asked. "I feel that we ought to do .. something for .. Papa .. soon."

She saw the expression on Lord Braydon's face and said quickly:

"I am not making that up. I can feel that he is suffering and perhaps he is in pain."

"Are you telling me they are torturing him?" Lord Braydon enquired.

"I .. I do not like to .. think of it, but I am sure it is the .. sort of thing they .. would do."

Lord Braydon's lips tightened, for he was sure that Loelia was in fact right in what she had said.

"I think it would be a mistake," he said after a moment, "for me to cancel my engagement for luncheon which I have already accepted. In fact, it is with the Captain of the '*Weissenburg*' so I hope I will learn something worth knowing."

He paused before continuing:

"In the meantime, use your own way of getting in touch with your father, and perhaps, although it seems very unlikely at the moment, we may both come up with something helpful."

"I am sure you will .. save Papa, I am .. sure you will!" Loelia said, "and I am so lucky that you are here. I know now that I would have been very .. ineffectual on .. my own."

Lord Braydon did not speak, but she knew what he was thinking and she said:

"You are quite right. I am desperately ashamed of myself for being so stupid as to come away without even a maid to look after me .. but I was so .. frantic to get to Papa."

She sighed and went on:

"There was no one in our household who would have been any good, and obviously I could not .. confide in .. anybody else."

"It is something you must never do again," Lord Braydon said, "and we can only hope that the Baron will keep quiet about last night and make sure that the woman in charge of the place where I found you keeps silent."

"I expect she will do anything for money," Loelia said in a low voice. "I am only distressed .. that you should have had to .. expend so much on .. me."

She looked lovely as she spoke shyly.

She was obviously so embarrassed that she should have cost him anything.

Lord Braydon smiled at her in a way that most women found irresistible.

"Forget it," he said, "and when we find your father I

shall tell him that in future he must look after you better."

"When you find him you can say anything you like!" Loelia said. "But let it be soon, very soon, or I have the terrifying feeling we may be .. too late!"

There was a little sob on the last two words.

As she walked away from him to stand looking out of the window Lord Braydon knew she was fighting against bursting into tears.

Remembering how she had cried against his shoulder last night after he had rescued her and he had felt her body trembling against his, he said angrily:

"You should be properly looked after!"

The sunshine turned Loelia's hair to gold.

He thought she was far too young and too lovely to be involved in anything so unpleasant and dangerous as her father's exploits.

"I must find out quickly where he is!" Lord Braydon said beneath his breath.

Then in a low voice, quite different from her ordinary one, Loelia said:

"He is in a .. tall house .. which has a pavement in front of it .. there are .. two sentries outside . . ."

Lord Braydon stared at her, but she did not turn around.

"Papa is .. down below ground-level .. it may be in a cellar .. it is a room with a long table in the centre of it and on the table are papers .. and I am .. sure Papa is expected to .. write something down .. or .. draw a plan."

"Can you see your father?" Lord Braydon asked quietly.

"No .. but I am aware that he is there .. I can .. feel him vibrating to me and .. he is thinking of me .. telling me what has .. happened and .. where he is."

Her voice died away and there was silence so that she turned round saying:

"Is that any .. help?"

"I am sure it will be," Lord Braydon said, "but unfortunately there are quite a number of Officials in this country who are important enough to have sentries outside their doors."

"If you could .. give me some names of people who own a house like that . . .?"

"We could not be sure of that," Lord Braydon said. "It may be the designer of the gun, or even the man who is the craftsman but neither of them would be authoritative enough to take your father prisoner."

Loelia gave a deep sigh, then she said:

"Please .. let me try .. you cannot be sure .. can you?"

It was impossible for Lord Braydon to give her the answer she obviously wanted.

"Of course not," he replied, "but if we work together, I am quite certain we can save your father."

He was speaking more optimistically than he really felt.

He was well aware that if Thurston Standish had been taken prisoner, the authorities would have made it almost impossible for him to escape or for anybody to rescue him.

To change the subject he said to Loelia:

"Tell me a little about your family. Although I have heard of your father and how brilliant he is, I really know nothing about him, and naturally I am interested as to why you are not better looked after in his absence."

Loelia smiled.

"Papa and I have always been the 'black sheep' of the family."

Lord Braydon looked surprised and she explained:

"My grandfather was determined that Papa, his only son, should go into his Regiment."

"Who is your grandfather?"

"He is General Sir Mortimer Standish-Drew!"

"Good Heavens!" Lord Braydon exclaimed. "I had no idea of that! I know your grandfather – of course I do! He was a hero when he retired, and everybody admired his brilliance in the campaigns he fought both in India and in Africa."

"Of course," Loelia agreed, "but Papa did not wish to follow his father blindly and do exactly what he was told."

She spoke slowly, as if she wanted him to understand as she could.

"He therefore decided when he was quite young that what he wished to do was to travel on his own, to learn languages, and eventually to write books about the strange people he met."

"And are his books going to be written for everybody else to read?"

"They will be when he publishes them."

"Do you mean to say he had already written them?"

"Two of them are written," Loelia replied, "and I helped him with them so I know they are much more thrilling than any other books I have ever read."

She saw the expression on Lord Braydon's face and said quickly:

"There are no secrets in them. Papa has all his secrets locked away until they are too out of date to make any trouble, and I am only afraid he will . . not be . . here to enjoy the success he will . . deserve as an author."

"You have not yet told me whether you have any other relatives who would be prepared to look after you."

Loelia smiled at him and he saw that she had a dimple on one side of her mouth.

"The truth is," she said, "that I am so happy with Papa that I have refused several aunts and cousins who have offered me a home with them."

She thought Lord Braydon might be disapproving and said quickly:

"Before Mama died she made me promise to look after Papa. Like all brilliant men, he never thinks of himself."

Her voice was very revealing as she went on:

"After he has completed his 'missions' as he calls them, he comes back looking emaciated through not eating the right food at the right time, and sometimes no food at all, and going for nights without sleep in order to bring off a successful coup."

"At the same time," Lord Braydon said gently, "I think you need somebody to look after you."

Loelia laughed.

"Think how boring it would be with them always saying to me: 'Do this, do that,' or saying as one of my aunts always does: 'You must try, Loelia dear, to behave like a lady!' "

She imitated the aunt in question so amazingly that Lord Braydon laughed in spite of himself before he asked:

"Is that very difficult?"

"I find it so. I do not want to be a society lady attending Balls and Receptions, and listening to the stupid conversations of young men who have done nothing more exciting than try to spot the winner of the Derby!"

Lord Braydon's eyes twinkled.

"You are being very scathing."

"I am telling the truth!" Loelia said defiantly. "After Papa, I find young men extremely stupid and incredibly boring. That is why I shall never marry!"

"You intend never to be married?" Lord Braydon asked incredulously.

"How could I bear to be tied to some man who has never known anything more dangerous than falling off his horse?"

As Lord Braydon did not reply she went on:

"A man who has never read a book since he left School, and who thinks that any young woman like myself should be overcome with gratitude that he condescends to speak to her!"

Lord Braydon threw back his head and laughed.

"It is all very well for you to laugh," Loelia said. "You know I am speaking the truth!"

She paused.

"In fact, when you were telling the Baron that fairy-story about the Lord-in-Waiting who wished to marry me, I could not help thinking that at least he might be more interesting than any of the young men I have met so far!"

"You can hardly expect me not to feel insulted by such a remark," Lord Braydon said.

Loelia looked at him.

He realised, incredible though it seemed, that she had not up to that moment thought of him as a young man.

On the train she had turned to him first for protection.

He was an Englishman and she knew him by name.

When he had saved her and carried her away from the House of Pleasure she had thought of him as an angel of deliverance.

She had not seen him as a living, breathing human man.

Lord Braydon saw this all so clearly without Loelia having to explain it in words, and he was surprised at himself.

He knew it was the truth.

Now as the colour rose in her pale cheeks he was aware she was embarrassed that he might be hurt by what she had said.

Then he added quickly:

"I am only teasing you, and I am not really insulted by your condemnation."

"B . . but . . I did not think about you like that," Loelia said. "I know you are . . very . . very clever and you behaved just as I know Papa would have done in the same circumstances."

Lord Braydon knew that, feeling the way she did about her father, she could not have said anything more flattering.

He was not speaking lightly as he replied:

"Thank you, Loelia! I only hope that in the future I will live up to your estimation of me."

CHAPTER FOUR

Lord Braydon went to the luncheon.

It proved to be fruitless and even more boring than the dinner-party had been the night before.

He had to answer a great many questions on the behaviour of the Prince of Wales on which he was determined to be non-committal.

His hosts were also curious about the Queen, who they spoke of with awe tinged with envy.

He found that all the Germans were suffering from frustration and a sense of inferiority because of the extent of the British Empire.

It seemed to creep into their conversation on every possible occasion.

Lord Braydon began to feel sick of defending Britain's position in the world.

When the luncheon was over he hurriedly returned to the apartment.

He was greeted with a cry of delight from Loelia as soon as he appeared.

"We have found it! We have found it!"

She held out to him a photograph taken at a Naval ceremony portraying a number of Admirals seated on deck with the Kaiser in the centre.

Loelia pointed to it.

There was no mistaking the appearance of a man in the back row.

He had a turned up moustache very much the same as the Emperor's with the exception, as she had said, that his was white.

Their names were printed at the foot of the photograph.

It confirmed that the man with the white moustache was in fact Eder Edersnier.

He had no 'von' before his name and was only a Commander, while nearly all the other men in the photograph were Admirals.

This made Lord Braydon sure that he had some special appointment in the German Navy.

He looked at the photograph for some time, committing the face to memory.

Then he said:

"You are quite certain this is the man you saw in your thoughts?"

"Absolutely certain!" Loelia replied.

"Where is Watkins?" Lord Braydon asked.

He was aware for the first time since he had come back from luncheon that Loelia was alone.

"After he found and brought me the photograph, he went out again to try to find where the Commander Edersnier lives."

Lord Braydon felt a sense of annoyance.

He very much disliked Watkins doing anything without orders or taking the initiative.

Loelia said quickly:

"You must not be angry with him. I was so . . impatient to get to Papa that I wanted to go and . . look . . myself, but he said that would make you . . angry."

"It certainly would!" Lord Braydon agreed.

"Once Watkins finds out where Papa is held prisoner, I shall have to discover some way of getting in touch with him."

"Now, let me make something clear from the very beginning,' Lord Braydon said firmly, "you will do absolutely nothing, unless I have given my approval to your plans."

His voice sharpened as he added.

"Moreover, I think it would be a great mistake for you to leave this apartment."

Loelia looked at him, then she said:

"I came to Berlin on .. my own to find .. Papa."

"And got into a terrible mess by doing so!"

He thought she was going to argue with him.

Instead she walked to the window to stand with her back to him looking out with sightless eyes at the sunshine.

Then after a moment she said in a low voice:

"You cannot .. stop me .. trying to .. save Papa."

"Of course not, and if you intend to do so on your own," Lord Braydon replied, "I suggest you go back to where I found you last night, and we can forget I was ever involved."

He spoke as he might have spoken to a recalcitrant recruit.

When Loelia turned to look at him he knew he had been cruel.

"How can you .. say that?" she asked, "when you know .. that if you had not come .. there as you .. did, I might at this .. moment be trying to .. kill myself."

She spoke in a very low voice, then ran to his side.

"Forgive me .. forgive me," she begged. "I should not have .. argued with you. It is only that I am so .. frantically worried about Papa. I know they are ill-treating him and .. trying to .. force him to do .. something it is .. impossible for him to do!"

She stood in front of Lord Braydon looking up into his face.

Because she was so contrite there were tears in her large eyes and her lips were trembling.

At the same time she looked so lovely that Lord Braydon had an almost irresistible impulse to put his arms around her and kiss her.

"It is not," he told himself, "because she is alluring like the Princess."

Actually she seemed to him at the moment little more than a child, a child who was caught up in a frightening nightmare and needed comforting.

He was sure, however, that Loelia had never been kissed by a man and she might easily misunderstand his intentions.

He therefore said in a quiet voice:

"I agree we must quickly find your father, but it is not going to help him or us if we quarrel or become over-dramatic."

Loelia drew in her breath.

"You are right . . of course you are right . . please forgive . . me."

"There is nothing to forgive," Lord Braydon said, "but we must sit down and think out what we must do, as soon as Watkins returns to tell us where the house is."

"I am sure he will say it is exactly as I have been able to see it," Loelia said. "At the same time, it would be helpful if I could . . stand outside it and try to get in touch with Papa. I am sure it would be easier to do so if I were nearer to him."

"I think it would be very unwise for you to stand outside the house," Lord Braydon said, "but perhaps we can drive past in a carriage."

"Could we do . . that?"

"I am sure it can be arranged," he replied.

As he spoke he heard somebody coming through the front-door of the apartment.

A second later Watkins joined them.

"I've found the house, M'Lord," he said. "It's in *Dahlern Strasse* and has two sentries, exactly as Miss Loelia described it."

He paused to grin at Loelia before he went on:

"There's a basement which the servants use, and below it there's a cellar."

"I was sure of that," Loelia murmured.

"I sees a grating level with the ground, M'Lord," Watkins continued, "and unless I'm mistaken, it'll be there to provide air to the cellar."

"A grating!" Loelia exclaimed. "If it were opened, could anyone get through it?"

"Not unless they was the size of a small child," Watkins replied.

Then he looked at Loelia as if he saw her for the first time and added:

"You might jus' manage it, Miss, if you could make yerself as thin an' sinuous as a snake."

"Now before we go any further," Lord Braydon interrupted, "Miss Loelia will not do anything such as you are suggesting. If we do make an attempt to rescue her father, she will wait here until we return with him."

"You cannot make me .. do that," Loelia protested indignantly, "not if I can be .. useful as Watkins .. suggests."

Watkins looked at his master.

"It'd be impossible for either you or me, M'Lord, to get into th' place through such a small opening, and I'd have thought too narrow even for Miss Loelia, slim as she is, except that from what she's bin tellin' me, she's bin used to climbin' in and out of strange places."

Lord Braydon looked at Loelia as if he thought she had been indiscreet.

"I was only telling Watkins of one or two adventures that Papa and I have had in the past," she said defensively.

She thought he looked annoyed, and went on quickly:

"Once for instance when we had been locked up by some bandits who wanted a ransom for us, I managed to escape up the chimney and found people to come and rescue Papa."

"Bandits are not the same as the Germans," Lord Braydon said. "They will shoot an intruder on sight and ask questions afterwards."

"If it is the only way to reach Papa, that is something I will have to risk," Loelia replied.

"It is a risk I will not allow you to take," Lord Braydon said firmly.

"How can you be so cruel as to let Papa be . . tortured by these . . people when perhaps we can get him . . away without their being . . aware of it?"

"Tell me how it is possible to do such a thing," Lord Braydon said scornfully. "You know already that there are sentries outside the house, and, I should imagine, innumerable servants inside. Moreover, if the gun is as important as we believe it to be, they will hardly leave it unguarded."

"The gun is not in that house," Loelia said in the soft, dreamy voice she used when she was seeing with her mind.

"Then why is your father there?"

"I think," she said slowly, "that perhaps Papa got near the gun, or they realised he knew too much. They are therefore trying to force him to tell them . . secrets of the British Navy before they . . kill him."

It was such an intelligent explanation that Lord Braydon could only stare at her in astonishment. But he said:

"This is only supposition, Loelia. We have nothing really concrete to assure us that your father is actually in the cellar."

"I know he is there . . I know it!"

She jumped up from the sofa on which she had been sitting and said:

"Please . . help . . please believe me . . I am not making up . . anything that I have told you . . it is true! It is as true as I am standing here . . and I will swear before . . God that I am not . . exaggerating the . . danger Papa is in and the need to . . save him quickly."

The sincerity with which she spoke was so convincing that Lord Braydon capitulated:

"Very well then," he said, "but if you are killed or taken prisoner, I hope it will not be on my conscience for the rest of my life."

"If the worst happens," Loelia said, "you must just forget me. After all, I came into your life by sheer chance because of that tiresome German on the train, and if I go out of it in the same unexpected manner, there will be . . no need for you to . . worry."

Lord Braydon had the feeling he would not only be worried, but he would find it impossible to forget Loelia.

But he thought there was no point saying so.

Looking at Watkins he asked quietly:

"How do you suggest we enter the Commander's house?"

"I've been thinkin', M'Lord, this is an opportunity to use them tablets you was given on our last exploit."

Lord Braydon raised his eyebrows.

He knew exactly what Watkins was referring to.

He had almost forgotten about some tablets he had been given by a Chinese Scientist in Hong Kong.

He had been involved in saving the Governor from being assassinated. The plot had been very unusual, and very complicated.

Lord Braydon had thought afterwards it was only by a stroke of sheer luck that he had been able to save the Governor's life.

He had also brought to justice a very unpleasant gang of criminals, who had been determined to seize power by any means however illegal.

What he had accomplished had been very much under cover. It was known only to the Foreign Secretary and recorded in a special file marked: *'TOP SECRET'*.

For his part in what had been a very risky operation, Lord Braydon had been presented with some special tablets by a Chinese Scientist.

He was told these might prove invaluable on some future exploit.

"I hope there will be no more like this one!" Lord Braydon had said positively.

"You never know, My Lord," the Scientist replied "and this is a discovery of which I am very proud."

"Tell me about it," Lord Braydon had said, knowing that was what he was expected to ask.

"These tablets dull a man's brain so that, while he

appears to the outside world to be completely normal and to be carrying on his ordinary affairs, whatever they might be, he is completely unaware of what is going on."

"I do not understand," Lord Braydon said.

"He becomes for a short time virtually a puppet, manipulated entirely by habit and not by the direction of his brain as a man is normally."

"It sounds extraordinary," Lord Braydon had remarked.

"It is!" the Scientist replied, "and what is additionally helpful is when the effects of the tablet wear off the person who has taken it has no idea that anything unusual has occurred."

"It certainly sounds a very useful thing to have in an emergency," Lord Braydon smiled.

He had accepted the tablets as a gift, knowing they were for the moment the Scientist's most prized possession.

He had never had occasion to use them.

Yet it was not surprising that Watkins had brought them with him on this trip to Germany, thinking they might be useful.

It was then that once again Lord Braydon's mind began to work like a well-oiled machine.

He knew as if he was telling himself a story exactly what they should do.

The first thing was to get himself invited to dinner by Commander Edersnier.

He got over that difficulty by once again using the Prince of Wales's name in a note, which was carried by Watkins to the house in the *Dahlern Strasse*.

He made it clear to the Commander that he was extremely anxious to see him before he left Berlin.

He said he had a message for him from the First Lord of the Admiralty and also from the Prince of Wales.

He therefore invited him, if it was not inconvenient, to a glass of wine after dinner in the apartment.

Then he wrote:

"You must forgive me that I cannot invite you to dinner, since I was not expecting to entertain in the short time I am here and have made therefore no culinary arrangements where I am staying.

But I am sure it would not be wise for us to talk together on such matters in any public place."

He knew this would at least intrigue the Commander, especially as he had marked his letter: '*Confidential and Personal*'.

Watkins, who waited for the answer, brought back the desired invitation to dine with the Commander.

He had also learnt, which was helpful, something about the inside of the house and the servants.

They were quite old and rather deaf.

He imagined they were employed by the Commander either because they had been with him for a long time or else were cheaper than servants in other houses.

That, Lord Braydon thought, was reasonable enough.

He was delighted to hear that when Watkins asked the Butler if he could have a drink while he was waiting, he had taken him down to the kitchen.

He had found it old-fashioned.

The only other servants were the cook, a scullery-boy and an old man who brought in the wood and coals for the fire.

"The cook tells me," Watkins said, "that she and the Butler, who's 'er 'usband, runs th' house for their master, and he's alone at the moment, his wife being in the country."

Lord Braydon thought that was most helpful and he therefore said as if he was talking to himself:

"I presume there will be quite a flutter at the thought of having a guest for dinner tonight."

"I'm sure o' that,' M'Lord," Watkins laughed. "In fact the Commander didn't seem too pleased about it when he handed me the note."

" 'Tell your Master,' he says to me, 'to be here sharp

at eight o'clock. It is difficult to have good food if people are late!' "

"What sort of man did he seem to be?" Lord Braydon enquired.

"Very German, M'Lord, and not a gentleman, so to speak."

Loelia, who was listening wide-eyed, said:

"I do not think the Commander is the man who has .. invented the gun, but I think .. perhaps he is in charge of the .. security surrounding it."

"I am prepared to agree with that," Lord Braydon said, "but of course we shall know more when we find your father."

She flashed him a smile that told him he had spoken as if he now assumed that was a certainty.

He thought her love for her father was very touching.

It struck him that very few women of his acquaintance would have been so intent on saving their father, their husband, or even their lover, as Loelia was.

She was even prepared to risk her own life in the attempt.

It was something he was to think of again.

At Loelia's insistence they hired a carriage and drove down the *Dahlern Strasse*.

Fortunately there was quite a lot of traffic, so that the carriage could go slowly past the house without attracting attention.

By the expression of Loelia's face Lord Braydon knew she was sending her thoughts to her father.

She was making absolutely sure that he was, as she had thought, inside the house and below the ground.

She did not speak until they were some minutes away from the house.

Then she said:

"He is there .. and I have a feeling he is .. growing weaker. If we do not .. save him tomorrow .. it may be too late."

As her voice trembled on the last word Lord Braydon took her hand in his.

"We will do our damndest – you must forgive my language – but we cannot do more."

"No . . of course . . not,' Loelia said.

Her fingers were trembling in his hand and he felt as if he held a small bird and it was fluttering with fear.

"What I am certain of," he said after a moment, "is that we must believe we will be successful, or we might create the wrong atmosphere."

Loelia turned to look at him in astonishment and said:

"You understand . . you really do . . understand!"

"I am trying to," he said. "Shall I say that I accept that you have exceptional powers of thought where your father is concerned."

Her fingers tightened on his as she said:

"While you are having dinner with the Commander, you will not forget to pray that Watkins and I are not heard?"

"I promise you I shall be doing that!" Lord Braydon said quietly.

. . . .

When Lord Braydon was dressed in his evening clothes he remembered he had no cape.

He certainly would not be able to retrieve it from where he had left it last night.

Watkins, however, was never at a loss.

He found a cape not unlike Lord Braydon's which belonged to the owner of the apartment.

He placed it on his master's shoulders saying:

"I'm sure, M'Lord, the gentleman won't mind us borrowing this, an' we can hardly tell 'm it's in a good cause!"

"For God's sake, Watkins, look after Miss Loelia," Lord Braydon said. "I feel I am very wrong to allow her to take part in this exploit, but I can think of no other way by which we can find out if she is right in believing that her father is a prisoner in that house."

"I don't mind betting me last farthin', M'Lord, that 'er's right," Watkins replied.

He spoke with an impertinence which on other occasions would have incurred a reprimand.

Now Lord Braydon merely added:

"If she is mistaken, get her away as quickly as possible."

"I'll do that, M'Lord."

"Make sure the coachman is trustworthy."

"We're paying too much for 'im to be anything' else!" Watkins replied. "An I've already instructed him to wait on the other side of the road under the trees. 'E won't see much from there."

Again Watkins had thought of everything.

Yet as Lord Braydon said good-bye to Loelia his instinct was to call the whole thing off.

He wanted to take her back to England where at least she would be alive and free from danger.

Never in any of his many adventures in the past had he ever been encumbered by the presence of a young woman.

He hoped it was something that would never happen again.

However he did not want Loelia to be aware of his fears, and having urged her to take care of herself he said:

"If anything goes wrong, just escape by any means you can and somehow get back here. Do you understand?"

"Of course I do," Loelia said, "and do not worry. I will try to reach Papa and tell him I am coming, so that he will be ready to help me once I have found him."

She spoke with a confidence that Lord Braydon wished he could share.

There was however nothing more he could do and he merely tried to smile at her before they all went downstairs.

Loelia was wearing a long coat which again they had borrowed from their host.

It was a man's coat and because she was so small it reached down to her ankles.

She looked slightly unusual but Lord Braydon hurried her through the hall where a porter was in attendance.

The carriage with its driver whom Watkins had said he could trust was outside.

As soon as they drove off Loelia took off the long coat she was wearing.

Lord Braydon lifted the lid of the box-seat for passengers sitting with their back to the horses.

Beneath the padded cushion on top of it was a space.

It could be used to store food for a long journey, or any valuables that a passenger was carrying.

There was just room for Loelia to squeeze inside.

She did so leaving the lid of the seat open.

Lord Braydon realised almost with a sense of shock that she was wearing a skin-tight garment like a diver's suit.

It revealed the outlines of her body and left her unencumbered by petticoats or skirt.

He was astonished by her garb, which he guessed had been provided for her by Watkins.

He was equally astonished that she was completely unselfconscious about it and made no attempt to apologise for her appearance.

It made him realise that she was very young.

She could, he thought, despite her beauty, have had very little to do with men in the past.

Those she had met had obviously been treated with contempt.

It had never occurred to her to be shy or in any way maidenly when she was engaged on something so serious as saving her father's life.

Lord Braydon knew that in fact he was more apprehensive than Loelia.

He was well aware of the terrible consequences which must ensue if their plot was discovered.

They pulled up outside the house and as he alighted from the carriage, Loelia disappeared into the box-seat.

The sentries presented arms and, Watkins having rung the bell, the door was opened by the aged Butler.

Lord Braydon was greeted effusively.

When he had gone inside the house and the door was shut Watkins said to the sentries:

"I wish I were gettin' a good dinner! I've bin on the go all day: 'Do this! Do that!' Never a time to 'ave a drink, let alone anythin' to eat!"

"I know what you are feeling," one of the sentries replied who was younger than the other. "It's hot standing here when the sun's out, and when the wind blows, it's cold."

All three men laughed as if it was a good joke and Watkins said:

"Tell you what – I'm going to 'ave a drink meself. There's a bottle in the back of th' carriage, an' I'll bring you boys a mugful. What d'you think o' that?'

There was a pause while the older sentry looked down the street.

It was deserted and under the trees there was no one to be seen.

There had been children with their nurses and boys playing ball earlier in the day, but now they had all gone home.

After a moment the sentry said:

"If we keeps our eyes skinned it'd be all right."

"That's wot I 'oped you'd say," Watkins replied. "I 'ates drinkin' alone. I'll move the carriage to the other side of the road, in case anyone's nosey enough to see what I'm doin'."

He signalled the driver to take the horses across under the trees.

Then he went to the back of the carriage where there was a hamper strapped between the wheels.

He opened it and poured himself a mug of claret from one bottle.

He drew two other mugs from the hamper and filled them from another bottle.

He carried the last two mugs across to the sentries saying:

"I'll fetch me own drink, then we'll 'ave a toast with no heel-tap."

They waited for him.

He returned with his own mug and the bottle of claret from which he had filled theirs.

He emptied his mug saying as he did so:

"To sweethearts! May they always be pretty and willing!"

The two Germans laughed at this.

Then as Watkins had suggested they gulped down the claret and he refilled their mugs as soon as they were empty.

He walked slowly back to the carriage and put the bottle of claret away in the hamper.

Then as he looked at the sentries he saw they had appeared to stiffen.

Although they held their mugs in one hand, their rifles were back on their shoulders.

He waited for about twenty seconds, then opened the door of the carriage.

Like a shadow Loelia slipped across the road and down the steps to the basement.

As she passed the sentries they never even glanced at her, and Watkins knew the drug had worked.

He removed the iron grating from its frame with a deftness that owed much to his own expertise.

He had a special instrument which he invariably took with him on his travels with Lord Braydon.

The aperture was small.

He knew that it was going to be a tight squeeze even for somebody as slim as Loelia.

But she had told him that she practised Yoga and had even learned a little Ju-Jitsu. This meant that she had complete control of her muscles.

Watkins realised she had not boasted when she went head first through the dark aperture.

By twisting and wriggling she managed to get her whole body through it.

It was then he knew he would have to cover her tracks.

Quickly he knocked very loudly on the door into the basement.

After a pause it was opened by the scullery-boy.

"Can I come in?" Watkins said cheerfully. "I thinks it'd be nice t' see you all again."

"You're very welcome, *Mein Herr!*" the Cook called from the kitchen, "but you must not interfere when I've to get this dinner ready with no one to help me, except Adolf, who's so heavy-handed he breaks everything he touches."

"Let me give yer a 'and," Watkins said, and settled down to do exactly that.

Talking loudly he drowned any noise that Loelia might make.

He had the Cook and scullery-boy laughing unrestrainedly.

When the old Butler came down from the Dining-Room in between the courses he joined in.

Watkins even carried a tray up to the Dining-Room door to save his legs.

He could hear Lord Braydon talking away about the yacht he said the Prince of Wales would like built which would beat '*Meteor II*'.

"I know, Commander, with your reputation for brilliant originality you could think of some way by which His Royal Highness can defeat his nephew."

"That is something the Emperor would not like," the Commander laughed, "but his uncle did not enjoy being beaten the year before last, or the quarrel they had before the Cowes week ended."

Both men laughed again as if it was a great joke.

Watkins peering through the crack in the door thought that Lord Braydon was eating each course as slowly as he could.

He was trying to stretch the dinner out as long as possible.

Watkins went back downstairs to help Cook with the apfelstrudel and the huge jar of cream that went with it.

"Your master and mine 'll be putting on weight if they guzzles all this!" he said.

The Cook laughed.

"Our Master's a poor eater, except when he has guests. In fact he'd forget his breakfast, luncheon and dinner if it were not for Friedrich reminding him it's on the table."

"That's wot 'appens with too much work," Watkins said sitting down comfortably at the table, "I makes it a rule never to exert meself, unless I 'as to."

"*Ach*, that's the British way," the Cook said. "We Germans are different. We like to keep on the go."

"And where does it get you?"

"You'd be surprised!" the Cook said ominously. "In fact one day, from all I hear, you'll be very surprised!"

"Well, you surprise me now with a good slice o' that dish that's just come downstairs," Watkins said, "an' I'll give you a kiss for your pains."

"*Ach*, get away with you, you saucy fellow!" Cook said. "You'll make Friedrich jealous!"

"And that'll keep him on the go!" Watkins quipped.

. . . .

Loelia could hear their laughter.

She groped her way through the darkness of the room she had entered through the now empty grating.

It was, she found, a cellar, empty except for some barrels which had once contained beer.

Loelia opened a door at the far end of it.

She found herself in another cellar, this time containing wine-racks which however held only a few bottles while there was room for a great many more.

She was beginning to feel that after all her thoughts had been mistaken and her father was not here.

Then she crossed a passage of flagged stones to a door on the other side.

It was very difficult to see what she was doing.

The only light and air came through the same sort of grating that Watkins had removed to let her into the house.

Here, however, there was a door in front of her.

As she reached it she realised there was a large key in the lock and a heavy bolt.

She quietly pulled back the bolt, and turned the key.

It was well-oiled and the door made no sound as she turned the handle.

It was then she prevented herself with difficulty from giving a cry of joy.

Sitting opposite her at a long table on which there were pads of paper was her father with his head in his hands.

For a moment she could only stand looking at him.

Then as if something told him he was not alone, he raised his head.

She saw with horror how emaciated he was.

CHAPTER FIVE

Thurston Standish did not speak.

He only rose from the chair on which he was sitting.

As Loelia ran round the table, he held out his arms.

She clung to him, aware that her heart was beating frantically.

There were a thousand things she wanted to say to him.

However she remembered he had taught her in the past that to speak, unless it was absolutely necessary was always dangerous.

He held her close for a long minute.

Then she took him by the hand aware that his fingers were very cold and drew him across the room.

She looked up and down the passage.

She was not expecting to see anyone, but making sure there was no one there.

Then as her father stepped out after her she locked the door.

She left the key in the lock just as she had found it.

Walking with the stealth of a Red Indian, as she had had to do more than once in the past, she went ahead.

Her father followed her up the stairs which she knew led to the basement.

This was the most dangerous part of their plan.

It would have been absolutely impossible for her father to leave by the grating through which she had entered the building.

Watkins had explained to her the plan of the floor above.

"There be," he said, "a long passage leadin' from th' outside door off which opens th' kitchen on one side o' it."

On the other side there was a pantry, a larder and beyond those, various storerooms.

He had drawn Loelia a plan to make quite sure she understood.

She reached the top of the stairs from the cellar.

She could hear laughter coming from the kitchen.

She knew that Watkins was keeping the servants amused so that they would not hear her father pass the door.

Moving with the swiftness of a young fawn, Loelia went ahead and reached the outer door.

She quickly opened it.

Her father joined her from the darkness at the top of the stairs.

As they let themselves out she knew he was drawing the fresh air into his lungs.

He was giving himself strength from it.

She shut the door again very quietly and hurried up the stone steps.

They passed through the gate in the railings which led into the road.

She paused for a moment to glance right and left to see if there were any passers-by.

So far as she could discern there were only the two sentries.

They were standing motionless at attention with their rifles on their shoulders.

The carriage was waiting under the trees.

The coachman, on Watkins' instructions she thought, was deliberately looking in the opposite direction.

Again moving with a swiftness that she could only pray her father could equal, she crossed the road.

She opened the carriage-door.

A few seconds later he joined her.

He got into the carriage and then, as she had half expected, collapsed on the back seat.

It was what Lord Braydon had anticipated might happen.

With an expertise which Loelia knew her father would admire she was ready to deal with the situation.

She helped him to lie down and covered him with a dark rug.

If anybody should look into the carriage they would not realise there was anyone beneath it.

Then she brought him first a drink.

Lord Braydon had prepared a very little brandy mixed with soda-water.

"Surely," Loelia had protested, "if Papa has had nothing to eat for a long time it will make him drunk?"

"What is more important," Lord Braydon said, "it will stimulate his appetite. When one has eaten nothing for perhaps weeks, it becomes hard to swallow and one no longer has any desire for food."

Loelia knew he was speaking sense.

As if her father understood this better than she did, he drank a little of the brandy which she held to his lips.

She knew it would have a quick effect.

After a few sips she put the glass down and opened a pot of Calves-Foot jelly.

She knew even better than Lord Braydon did that it was the most nourishing substance it was possible to obtain.

It was used for invalids and convalescents who were unable to swallow or digest any more solid form of nourishment.

Slowly she spooned it into her father's mouth.

She thought that as he swallowed it obediently, a little more colour came into his face.

Although his eyes were closed she knew he was alert and aware of the danger they were in.

When the small pot was practically finished, she gave him a little more of the brandy.

Then covering him completely with the rug she looked expectantly through the window across the road.

. . . .

As dinner finished and the coffee had been taken up to the Dining-Room, Watkins glanced up at the clock.

It was a large one ticking on the kitchen-wall.

"It's after nine o'clock."

He said to the old Butler.

"You'd better go to the Drawing-Room and remind 'Is Lordship 'e's promised to be with her Highness the Princess Von Achern in ten minutes."

"You're not giving him much time to get there!" Friedrich remarked.

"All th' more reason for 'Is Lordship to hurry!" Watkins replied.

Friedrich moved slowly from the kitchen.

Watkins said goodbye to the Cook, kissing her on both cheeks which made her giggle like a young girl.

He gave the scullery-boy and the old man a generous tip each.

It made them speechless with gratitude.

Then, jauntily telling the staff he would be seeing them again, he went from the kitchen.

He shut the door behind him and walked down the passageway.

As he went he was hoping that all had gone well.

By now Miss Loelia should have taken her father to safety.

If, contrary to her expectation her father was not there he knew she would not have been so foolish as to linger about.

She would have returned, as Lord Braydon had instructed her, to the carriage.

As he reached the door of the basement steps he saw the sentries still standing woodenly at attention.

He was aware that they each of them held in their free hand the mug from which they had drunk the drugged claret.

He collected the two empty mugs.

They took no notice of him as he did so, merely staring ahead.

It was the way they had been taught to do when they first came on sentry-duty.

Carrying the mugs Watkins hurried across the road. He put them into the hamper at the back of the carriage and then went up to the door.

One glance through the window told him that all was well.

He stood outside waiting for Lord Braydon to appear.

. . . .

Lord Braydon had in fact been waiting tensely for Watkins' message to be brought by the Butler.

When he heard it he said to the Commander:

"You must forgive me if I leave you now, and I must say it is with reluctance, but as I am leaving Berlin tonight, I have promised to say goodbye to Princess Von Achern before I go."

"You are leaving tonight, *Mein Herr?*"

"Sadly," Lord Braydon replied. "It is a Royal Command which I cannot ignore."

"I understand," the Commander said.

"You will promise to communicate with me as soon as possible about our discussion?" Lord Braydon asked. "I shall be waiting anxiously for your letter and so, may I add, will His Royal Highness."

"I will go into the matter thoroughly," the Commander replied pompously, "but it may be difficult, as I know you are aware."

"A difficulty which I only hope you can overcome," Lord Braydon smiled as he walked to the front-door.

Friedrich was there to put his cape over his shoulders and received a golden coin for doing so.

Going outside, Lord Braydon said:

"I see my coachman has been sensible enough to park the horses under the trees. Now goodbye, and thank you more than I can say for your hospitality."

He shook the Commander warmly by the hand.

Then he hurried across the road towards the carriage, Watkins opened the door to let him in.

The look on his face was enough to tell Lord Braydon that all had gone well.

Only as they drove off did Loelia throw back the lid of the box-seat.

She had hidden herself in case the Commander decided to accompany Lord Braydon to the carriage.

"We have . . done it! We have done . . it!" she said in a whisper.

Lord Braydon was sitting on the very edge of the back-seat so as not to crush Thurston Standish's legs.

"Good girl!" he said. "How is your father?"

"Very grateful!" Thurston Standish murmured.

He pushed the rug back from his face, but was still lying stretched out.

"I am delighted to see you!" Lord Braydon said.

Thurston Standish managed a faint smile as he replied.

"I know who you are, and I have been hoping that Loelia would find somebody like you to help her to rescue me."

"You knew that was what she intended to do?" Lord Braydon asked.

"Yes, I knew!" Thurston Standish said quietly.

Loelia who had meanwhile emerged from the box, went down on her knees beside him.

"I love you, Papa," she said, "and I have been so . . desperately afraid that we might be . . too late. But Lord Braydon has been . . wonderful!"

"Do not let us speak too soon!" Lord Braydon warned. "When they find your father gone they will make every effort to get him back."

"Perhaps you had better tell me at once what you plan to do," Thurston Standish interposed.

"I will do that," Lord Braydon agreed, "but first I hope you have eaten some food because I can see they have starved you."

"I will tell you all about that later," Thurston Standish said.

He was unable to say more.

Loelia had opened another pot of calves-foot jelly and was spooning it into his mouth.

She was aware as she did so that Lord Braydon was looking at her father anxiously.

He was afraid that the older man would not be capable of carrying out the next stage of his plan.

When they arrived back at the apartment house, only he and Loelia entered through the front-door.

Watkins drove with the carriage round to the back.

Going up in the lift alone with Lord Braydon she said in a tremulous voice:

"Do you think Papa will be able to do all you expect of him? He looks dreadfully tired and weak."

"I think your father's will-power will carry him over the next hurdle," Lord Braydon said, "which in a way is the most important of all. It is not going to be easy to get out of Germany once the hue and cry for him starts."

"I know . . that."

As Loelia spoke she trembled.

Without thinking she slipped her hand into Lord Braydon's.

"We cannot . . fail now," she said in a desperate little voice.

"It is impossible for us to fail!" Lord Braydon said firmly.

She knew he was trying to give her courage and strength.

Having reached her bedroom, Loelia quickly changed into the clothes she had left ready on a chair.

She stuffed the garment she had been wearing into her suitcase.

She had only just finished doing so when there was a knock on the door.

It was Lord Braydon, who also had changed into his travelling-clothes and looked exceedingly smart.

There was a porter behind him with his trunk.

He picked up the suitcase which Watkins had bought for Loelia at the market.

It contained the few other garments he had purchased at the same time as those she was now wearing.

Lord Braydon looked at his watch and said for the purpose of impressing it on the porter:

"We shall have to hurry. I must see the Princess, and our train leaves at eleven o'clock."

"I am ready," Loelia replied.

The porter hurried away to the Service-lift and they went down in the one they habitually used.

By the time they reached the hall the porter was already there and carrying the luggage to the carriage.

Now the hamper had been removed from the box and the cases were put in its place.

Loelia was aware that Watkins had not moved from the box of the carriage but was leaving everything to the porter.

Lord Braydon tipped the man generously.

He stepped into the carriage where Loelia was already sitting on the front edge of the back-seat in order to conceal her father behind her.

Only as they drove off did Lord Braydon ask anxiously:

"You are all right, Standish?"

"You need not worry about me," Thurston Standish replied. "Your man has told me what is expected of me, and I will certainly do my best to look like an efficient 'Gentleman's gentleman'!"

Lord Braydon laughed.

Then as the horses moved on he said:

"Did Watkins give you anything to cover up the pallor of your face?"

"If he had not done so, I would have thought of it myself!" Thurston Standish replied.

There was just a touch of rebuke in his voice, as if he thought Lord Braydon was accusing him of not knowing the art of disguise.

"As you can imagine," Lord Braydon said in a low

voice, "this whole operation is going to be very tricky from now on."

"It was very clever of you," Thurston Standish said, "to call on the Princess. It will make the Germans think, when they start investigating your movements, that you would not have done so had you been in a hurry to spirit me out of the country."

"That is what I thought myself," Lord Braydon said, "and also I left, accidentally, as I hope they will think, on the desk in my apartment a note from the British Embassy."

There was a note of amusement in his voice as he continued:

"It says they had been informed by London that Her Majesty requires my presence immediately as His Highenss the Maharajah has arrived earlier than was anticipated from India."

Thurston Standish gave a little laugh as he said:

"I have always heard how intelligent you were, Braydon! There is nothing more effective in this country than to play a 'Court card' if you have one."

"That is what I thought," Lord Braydon said. "When we are out of trouble, I will tell you how much I admire you, and always have done."

"I hope I shall not now 'blot my copy-book'," Thurston Standish said.

As he spoke he lay down again and covered himself with the dark rug.

. . . .

Watkins left the footman at the Princess's very palatial house to open the carriage-door for Lord Braydon.

As he did so he turned to Loelia in English:

"I will not be long, my dear."

Then in German to the coachman:

"Wait here! I shall be only a few minutes."

As he went into the house the footman shut the carriage-door.

Loelia, who was sitting erect with her father lying behind her asked:

"Are you all right Papa? Do you feel better?"

"I have been eating all the time while Watkins has been dressing me and giving me my instructions."

"I am sure he has done it very efficiently," Loelia said, "so there is no need for me to say anything."

She spoke in a whisper.

She knew that the footman who had retired inside the lighted door of the Princess's house believed her to be alone.

"I am proud of you, my darling," Thurston Standish said, "but you should not have taken such an appalling risk as to come to Berlin alone."

"I will tell you all about that later," Loelia said hastily.

She knew how upset her father would be when she told him exactly what had happened.

For the moment she wanted him to think of nothing but Lord Braydon's plan of escape.

. . . .

Inside the house the Princess, looking even more alluring that Lord Braydon remembered, gave an exclamation of dismay when she saw how he was dressed.

"You are not leaving?" she exclaimed.

Lord Braydon had sent her a letter earlier explaining that owing to a commitment which he could not avoid he would be unable to dine with her.

He had however promised to call on her after dinner.

He knew she would assume they would be able to enjoy the *tête-à-tête* she had envisaged once they were alone.

Holding her hand in his for longer than was necessary Lord Braydon replied:

"I cannot tell you how upset and distressed I am, but just before dinner I received a communication from the Embassy to say that Her Majesty wished me to return to London immediately.

"A Maharajah from India is arriving who she has arranged for me to entertain during his visit to England."

The Princess pouted and her red lips were very enticing.

"How could Fate be so unkind to us?" she asked in a low voice.

"What do you think I am feeling?" Lord Braydon asked.

His fingers tightened on hers before he said:

"There will be other times and other meetings, but tonight, as the train carries me away, you know of whom I shall be thinking."

He sounded so sincere that the Princess drew in her breath as she said:

"Then after all it is only *'au revoir'* and not good-bye."

"That is always true where we are concerned," Lord Braydon said and kissed her hand.

It was impossible to say more.

He knew the Princess's guests at the other end of the room were trying to talk naturally amongst themselves.

At the same time they were casting curious glances to where their hostess was standing just inside the door.

"You are more beautiful than ever," Lord Braydon said softly and kissed the Princess's hand once again.

Then he left.

He stepped back into the carriage.

As they drove away Loelia asked curiously:

"Is the Princess very beautiful?"

"Very!" Lord Braydon replied dryly.

But he did not say any more.

She told herself he was bound to be disappointed and perhaps angry that he could not spend the evening as he had intended.

'He must think that Papa and I are a terrible nuisance,' Loelia told herself. 'He must wish he never met me and will be delighted, once we are back in England, that he need never see me again!'

She found this thought distressing in a manner she did not understand.

She looked at Lord Braydon in the light of the gas-lamps as they flashed past them.

She thought that no one could look more handsome, more elegant, or be more intelligent.

She knew that even if she never saw him again she would always remember him.

Suddenly, before they reached the station, the horses came to a standstill.

For a moment Loelia had the frightening idea that something had gone wrong.

Supposing the Police wished to check on anyone who was with Lord Braydon?

Then she remembered his plan.

She knew that this was the point at which Watkins was to leave them.

He climbed down from the box of the carriage.

As soon as he reached the ground the horses drove on.

She had a quick glimpse of him.

He looked very different from the way he usually did, wearing a cap on his head instead of his usual smart bowler.

He was also pulling off his mackintosh. Under it he was wearing a vulgar check suit with a yellow tie and carried a holdall.

"Will he be all right?" Loelia asked Lord Braydon a little anxiously.

He smiled.

"One person I never worry about is Watkins," he replied. "There is nothing he enjoys more than what he looks on as an adventure, and at the end of it, however dangerous he always comes up smiling."

As he spoke he said to the man lying behind him:

"I think, Standish, you should now sit on the small seat and take up your part."

"Of course," Thurston Standish agreed with a touch of amusement in his voice. "I was merely awaiting instructions."

He raised himself slowly, and with some difficulty moved across the carriage.

Loelia sat on the back seat beside Lord Braydon.

Then as he looked at her father she wanted to laugh.

She knew it was Lord Braydon's idea that he should take Watkins' place as his valet.

Although she had seen him before in various disguises, she had not expected him to look so exactly the picture of a valet.

His high white collar and black tie, the black suit which Watkins had been wearing and which was too large for him, were exactly right.

It was, Loelia knew, the accepted 'uniform'.

Her father had parted his hair in the middle.

His face was not made up except for a little colouring to attempt to conceal his emaciation.

He had immediately assumed the facial expression of a servant who was there to obey orders and was anxious to please.

Watkins' bowler hat was on the seat beside him.

When he put it on after arriving at the station, Loelia would have laughed, if she had not been so frightened that they would not get away.

Lord Braydon had arranged that a Courier from the British Embassy would be waiting.

He escorted them to their sleeping-compartments and handed over their tickets.

He was rather a pompous man who ignored Lord Braydon's 'valet'.

He had, however, been efficient enough to have a porter waiting by his side as the carriage drew up outside the station.

"I am afraid I have given you very short notice to make arrangements for me," Lord Braydon said courteously.

"Fortunately, My Lord, the train was not over-booked, and I have reserved three compartments in the centre of a sleeping-car so that you will not be over the wheels."

He continued slowly.

"I have also arranged, as you requested, that both your Ward and your valet are next to you."

"Thank you," Lord Braydon replied.

They set off in a little procession.

The Courier walked beside Lord Braydon with Loelia, followed by the 'valet'.

The porter brought up the rear with the luggage.

As they boarded the train Lord Braydon thanked the Courier for his attention.

He then told him there was no reason for him to wait.

"I am sure you have a great deal to do at the embassy," Lord Braydon said, "and I can only apologise for keeping you out so late."

"It has been a pleasure, My Lord."

Lord Braydon shook him by the hand and Loelia did the same.

As she did so she saw a man walking down the platform towards the Second Class compartments.

She would not have recognised Watkins if she had not been looking out for him.

Lord Braydon said he was to be an American tourist.

He had produced by some magical means of his own a passport giving Watkins' name as Kirk Webber.

"You are to say that you have come home to see the land of your fathers," Lord Braydon had told him, "and be very voluble about the wonders of the Fatherland to anybody who will listen to you."

Now as Loelia saw Watkins swaggering down the platform she thought he was an excellent actor.

Even the most astute German would find it hard to believe he was a polite, obsequious valet.

While they were saying goodbye to the Courier, she was aware that her father was assiduously unpacking Lord Braydon's night-attire.

Anyone looking through the window of the sleeper would have thought that he was only carrying out the duties for which he was paid.

Going to her own sleeper, Loelia was praying frantically that they would not be stopped.

Also that by some miracle the Commander was not yet

aware that his prisoner had escaped.

It seemed a century of time until the guard had blown his whistle and waved his red flag.

The wheels began to turn and she moved from her own sleeper into Lord Braydon's next door.

There she found, as she had expected, that he and her father were together.

When they were clear of the platform they sat down on the bed and heaved a sigh of relief.

It was then that Loelia put her arms around her father and kissed him.

"We have done it! Oh . . Papa . . we have done it! Tell me that . . you are all right . . I have been so desperately afraid I would not . . reach you in time!"

"I am all right, my darling," he said, "but if His Lordship will excuse me, I want to lie down."

"Yes, of course," Loelia said.

"I have some more food for you," Lord Braydon said, "which is in my case, and I also think it would do us good to have a glass of champagne. I suggest you go to your compartment while I summon a steward."

He smiled as he continued:

"At the same time I will tip him generously so that if there are any enquiries about us at the frontier he will certainly give us a good reference!"

Thurston Standish gave a weak little laugh.

Without saying any more he went to his compartment which was next to Loelia's.

She followed him saying as they went inside:

"Let me help you, Papa."

He shook his head.

"That might be a mistake: I am His Lordship's valet and it is something we must not forget until we are outside this country."

She knew he was talking sense.

She merely kissed him, then went to her own compartment to wait for Lord Braydon.

He brought her a glass of champagne.

When no one was about he took a glass into the sleeper next door and with it some pâté sandwiches. Loelia knew it was the sort of luxury the steward would expect a nobleman to enjoy at this time of night.

When he came back he said:

"Your father is already in bed and tells me that in the circumstances he is feeling much better than he expected."

"Did he tell you anything else?" Loelia asked.

Lord Braydon hesitated as if considering whether he should answer truthfully or not.

Then he replied:

"Your father was tortured to start with, but then he was clever enough to persuade them that unless he kept his faculties about him he would be unable to do what they asked, even if he were willing to do so."

"What did they want him to do?" Loelia asked.

"As you know, I have not yet had a chance to question your father, and it would be a mistake to do so until we are on neutral territory."

Loelia had to be content with that.

As she sipped her champagne Lord Braydon sat down beside her and said:

"I suppose you know you have been completely and absolutely magnificent! I never believed any woman could have behaved as you have done and at the same time be so brave!"

The way he spoke made Loelia blush and she felt too shy to meet his eyes.

"You are very beautiful, Loelia," Lord Braydon said. "I think this sort of life is a mistake for somebody who should be shining in the social world and not worrying about international intrigue."

"You know what I think about the . . social world!"

"Of which you obviously know very little," Lord Braydon retorted. "When I tell your father of the lies we invented for Baron Von Krozingen, we should make them come true."

He smiled at her.

"I will find one of my relatives, perhaps my grandmother who *is* the Duchess of Exmouth to present you and make you the social success you ought to be."

"No . . no!" Loelia cried. "That is something which does not . . interest me. I would much rather be taking part in . . adventures like this . . although they are frightening . . with Papa . . and . . with you."

There was a little pause before the last two words and Lord Braydon asked curiously:

"You have really enjoyed being with me?"

"Of course I have!" Loelia replied quite unselfconsciously. "I did not know that there were . . men like you in the world."

"What do you mean by that?"

She looked away from him as she said:

"You are rich . . important . . you have houses, racehorses . . and a great many social friends. Why should you be concerned with the sort of . . missions which intrigue and . . excite Papa?"

"I suppose for the same reasons you have just attributed to him – they intrigue and excite me!"

"But . . we are not rich, so Papa has little else in his life . . while you have . . everything you could . . possibly want."

"It may sound greedy," Lord Braydon replied. "But I want more than luxury and amusement. Perhaps if I were married with a family it would be different, but although you may not believe it, I am often bored with a surfeit of *pâté de foie gras*!"

Loelia laughed.

"Is that how it feels to you? I have often wondered if one can have too much of everything that is beautiful and luxurious."

"I can assure you," Lord Braydon replied, "it is quite easy to find that 'familiarity breeds contempt'."

"That is wrong . . quite wrong . . I am sure you have not explored all the other things you might do in your position."

He looked at her in surprise.

"What are you suggesting?"

"You are a member of the House of Lords and there are so many reforms which are vitally necessary in the country. So many injustices that should be brought into the open and thus eliminated."

Lord Braydon looked at her in sheer astonishment.

She had taken off her hat and her hair seemed like sunshine against the dark panelling of the sleeper.

Her skin was a translucent contrast to the lady-like gown which Watkins had bought for her.

He was aware that she was really beautiful, but in a different way from any woman he had known before.

He knew it was because she had an aura.

He thought it was a mixture of youth, purity and spirituality.

He was already aware of how unselfconscious she was and that her devotion to her father was unusual and very touching.

Abruptly, because it came suddenly to his mind, he asked:

"What do you intend to do when we get back to England?"

"Papa and I will go home."

"Do you realise I have no idea where that is?"

She smiled at him.

"It is north of London, in a village in Hertfordshire. We live in a small Manor House with a few acres of land on which we keep horses, but that is all."

She made a gesture that was very eloquent as she said:

"Can you really imagine that being enough to hold Papa's interest when he is so brilliant at languages? He understands the complexities of so many countries in the world, and has so much to give to other people."

She glanced at Lord Braydon to see if he was interested, then she went on:

"It was different when Mama was alive. They were so happy together that nothing else was of any importance."

She smiled at him then went on:

"Although I have tried to take her place, life for him can never be the same . . without her."

"I can understand your father feeling like that," Lord Braydon said in a different voice, "but I am thinking of you."

"I shall . . be all . . right."

"And you will stay alone while your father goes a-roving?"

"There is quite a lot for me to do at home."

"With no one to admire you?"

She smiled.

"The horses love me. They come when I call them, and I am very happy when I am riding."

"I would like to show you my horses."

He saw Loelia's eyes light up.

"I would love to see them! I believe your stables at Bray Park are among the best in England!"

"Who told you that?"

"I think I read it in one of the illustrated Magazines, and there was a picture of your house. It is very big."

"Very big," Lord Braydon agreed, "and like your father, I often feel lonely, which again answers your question as to why I do what I do."

"But . . it is . . dangerous," Loelia murmured.

"If I am in any danger in the future," Lord Braydon smiled. "I shall think of you and try to reach your thoughts, so that you will be able to help me!"

He had meant to tease her.

But she looked at him with her strange eyes and said quietly:

"That is . . something I would . . like to do."

CHAPTER SIX

Loelia lay awake long after she was in bed in her sleeper.

She was thinking over everything that had happened.

The wheels of the train told her her father was free.

At the same time she was apprehensive of what might happen when they reached the Frontier.

Lord Braydon in his own inimitable way had given them his orders.

"It would be a mistake," he said, "for us to be up and dressed and looking as if we thought we might be questioned."

"Do . . you think we . . will be?" Loelia asked with a tremble in her voice.

"I am certain that by this time," Lord Braydon said quietly, "Edersnier will have found that his prisoner has escaped. He will certainly notify the Secret Police and anybody else concerned with your father's activities."

He saw the colour drain away from Loelia's face.

He added in a different tone:

"But I cannot believe Fate or the gods would have allowed us to get this far only to fail now."

"No . . of course not," she replied.

He saw the light come back into her eyes.

She must have dozed off just a few minutes before the train came to a rumbling halt.

As her heart missed a beat she knew they had reached the Frontier.

Despite what he had said to reassure Loelia Lord Braydon was feeling very anxious.

However, he lay relaxed in his sleeper.

His eyes were closed, until there came a demanding rap on his door.

He ignored it and the knock came again and now an authoritative voice said:

"Open, if you please, *Mein Herr!*"

Grumbling beneath his breath, but deliberately loud enough to be heard, Lord Braydon stumbled from his bed to the door.

He unlocked it and opened it a crack.

"What is it?" he enquired.

"Your papers, please, *Mein Herr!*"

"Oh, for God's sake!" Lord Braydon exclaimed in English. "Why do you want to see them at this hour of the night?"

He left the door open, however.

Going to the pocket of his coat he pulled out a leather wallet and flung it on the bed.

"There you are!" he said. "You will also find there the papers concerning my Ward who is next door, and my valet who is in a compartment further on, so there is no need for you to disturb them."

The official, who he realised was a Senior Officer, gave him a sharp glance.

Lord Braydon yawning loudly got back into bed and leaning back against his pillows shut his eyes.

Very slowly and precisely the Official looked at the three passports, then said:

"I understand, *Mein Herr*, that you dined last night with Commander Edersnier."

Lord Braydon opened his eyes.

Then after a pause, as if he was collecting his thoughts he said:

"Edersnier! – yes, of course – as you say I dined with him."

He stiffened.

"What has that to do with you?" he asked sharply.

"My visit to the Commander was private, and my reason for being there is my affair and nobody else's."

The way he spoke was exactly the way in which the officer's own superiors would have spoken to him.

Almost apologetically he explained.

"I have to ask these questions, *Mein Herr*, because I am informed by Headquarters that a prisoner has escaped who was in the Commander's custody."

"A prisoner? What do you mean – prisoner?" Lord Braydon asked. "The Commander and I dined alone in his private house, and if he was holding prisoners in another part of the City, I was of course, not aware of it."

The Official was obviously taken aback by his tone and after a moment he said:

"I have been instructed, *Mein Herr*, to ask if you would help the Naval Police with their enquiries."

"What you are asking is impossible!" Lord Braydon replied. "Kindly inform the Police that I am returning to England, having received an official summons via the British Embassy that Her Majesty the Queen requires my services immediately at Buckingham Palace."

His voice sharpened.

"It would therefore be out of the question for me to delay my journey, if I wished to do so, even for a few hours."

The Official to whom he was speaking looked indecisive.

Lord Braydon was sure that he was not important enough to assert any jurisdiction over him.

He therefore hesitated and was lost.

"I have nothing more to say," Lord Braydon announced.

He spoke in a lofty, overwhelming voice which was very unlike the usual way in which he spoke.

"Tell your superiors that they can contact me at any time through the German Ambassador in London. He knows my address and is in fact a personal friend. At the moment, I have no time to look for, or discuss, prisoners about whom I know nothing whatsoever!"

His voice was commanding, as he said:

"Make that very clear – I have no knowledge of what you are speaking, and my contact with Commander Edersnier was entirely in connection with a racing yacht."

There was nothing the Official could do but put down the passports which he held in his hand.

With a somewhat awkward bow he said:

"I understand, *Mein Herr*, and please excuse my interruption, but I am of course carrying out my orders."

"Yes, yes!" Lord Braydon said. "Shut the door. I cannot be bothered to get out of bed to lock it again."

He yawned as he spoke and looked convincingly tired and bored as he did so.

The Official shut the door.

There was a long whispered conversation with two other officials and the steward as to whether they should wake Loelia.

Her passport claimed her to be Miss Johnson.

Lord Braydon could not hear exactly what they were saying.

But he knew from his tone of voice that the steward was assuring them there was nothing sinister or in any way suspicious about the three people who had boarded the train in Berlin.

Finally the German officials seemed to accept what he said.

However, they took a long time in doing so, and moved away down the corridor.

The train waited for a long time at the Frontier.

Lord Braydon did not move although he was aware that Loelia and her father would be as anxious as he was.

He was afraid that they were still suspicious and were trying to obtain further instructions from Headquarters.

At last the wheels once again began to turn.

Only as the pace of the train quickened did he feel an irrepressible relief sweep over him.

He felt that he must speak to Loelia and make sure she was no longer afraid.

If he was honest, he had been terrified that at the last moment they would not get away.

He put on a long silk robe which Thurston Standish had dutifully laid out for him.

He knew there would be another stop when they reached the Dutch frontier.

But as he expected, this was just a formality and the Dutch waved the train through without disturbing the occupants.

It was then that Lord Braydon went out into the corridor and knocked on Loelia's door.

"W .. who .. is it?"

He knew by the question that she was trembling and he replied in English:

"I am asking if you are all right."

He heard her pull back the lock and the door opened a little.

He saw that she was wearing nothing over her nightgown.

Her eyes, dark with fear, seemed to fill her whole face.

He smiled at her.

"I only came to tell you," he said, "that now we are free and the bogeys are all left behind!"

He was trying to make her smile.

But she said almost like a child who had been frightened by the dark:

"You are .. sure .. you really are .. sure? I .. I heard that man talking to you .. for so long that .. I was .. frightened .. very frightened."

"Of course you were," he replied.

He swayed a little with the movement of the train and asked:

"May I come in for a moment? I have no wish to disturb your father who I hope is sleeping but I think we should make plans concerning what we do when we reach Ostend."

Loelia did not reply. She merely moved back into her sleeper and got into bed.

Lord Braydon came in, closed the door and sat down on the end of the bed.

He saw she was looking at him still anxiously, and he said:

"It is really all right, and I think I convinced them that none of us has any knowledge of an escaped prisoner."

She gave a deep sigh which seemed to come from the very depths of her being before she said:

"Perhaps it was foolish of me to have been so .. frightened .. but I have not only .. Papa to worry about this but .. you too. After all, you were .. dragged into this .. and it was something that should not have .. happened."

"I think without me you might have found it more difficult to get your father away!" Lord Braydon remarked.

"I did not mean that," Loelia said quickly. "You were magnificent, marvellous .. no one could have been so wonderful."

She hesitated, and said softly:

"But if we had got you into trouble .. it would have been .. something for which Papa and I would have been .. desperately sorry for the rest of our lives."

The way she spoke told Lord Braydon that it meant a great deal to her.

After a moment he said quietly:

"I want you to forget everything that has happened and in the future enjoy yourself."

"I am prepared to do that," Loelia said, "but I have no wish .. to do what .. you suggested."

She gave him a nervous little glance before she said:

"I must look after Papa and besides, as I have already told you, I do not .. fit into the social world."

"I understand your feeling like that," Lord Braydon said, "but I still think it is a terrible waste to be restricted in a small house with only a few acres of land."

"Now you are quoting . . my words . . against me!" Loelia said accusingly.

"If you want *me* to expand *my* horizons," Lord Braydon said, "I think we should broaden *yours*."

She made a helpless little gesture with her hands as she said:

"I think the truth is I am 'neither fish nor flesh nor good red herring!' as my Nanny used to say. In other words, I do not fit in . . anywhere!"

"Now you are being ultra-modest," Lord Braydon said, "but that is something we can talk about another time. Now I am going to sleep, and I suggest you do the same thing."

He smiled at her as he rose to his feet.

Then before he left the compartment he turned back briefly to say:

"Just remember, Loelia, we have been successful where other people not as clever as we are might have failed."

He smiled at her again, shut the door and went back to his own sleeper.

Lord Braydon made no effort to rise until the steward called him.

He informed him that breakfast was being served in the Dining-Car and that they would be arriving in Antwerp in an hour's time.

Lord Braydon had no intention of going to the Restaurant car just in case he should see somebody he knew.

He would then have to explain why Loelia was travelling with him.

He was well aware of the construction most people would put on her presence in his company without a chaperone.

He also knew that it would never for a moment cross her mind that there was anything wrong in their being together.

He therefore ordered breakfast for himself in his compartment, and the same for her.

He was sure that Thurston Standish would take care of himself.

In fact it was only just before the train came into Antwerp that he came into Lord Braydon's compartment.

He was still dressed as a valet, and looked a good deal better than he had the day before.

He carefully shut the door before he spoke.

Then he said:

"As your valet I sincerely apologise for over-sleeping after we passed the Frontier."

Lord Braydon smiled at him.

"I thought you would be lying awake wondering what was happening, and I admit to having been nervous myself."

He then told Thurston Standish exactly what had been said:

"I think we are out of the wood," he added, "but it would be a great mistake for the steward to have grounds for thinking we have behaved any differently from what he expected of us, until we are on board my yacht, which I hope we shall find waiting for us in the harbour."

Thurston Standish agreed with him and therefore began deftly to pack his things.

He then went next door to collect Loelia's case.

By this time they were coming into the station.

Loelia understood from the glance her father gave her that she was still to behave as if he actually was the valet he pretended to be.

She therefore stepped out onto the platform with Lord Braydon.

They left Thurston Standish to find a porter for their luggage and follow them as they went towards the harbour.

They saw Lord Braydon's yacht moored on to a different quay from the Cross-Channel Steamer and flying the White Ensign.

It looked so unmistakably British that Loelia felt it was impossible to walk slowly towards the gangway.

She wanted to run, knowing that once aboard the yacht she would at last feel really safe and no longer menaced.

Thurston Standish tipped the porter who brought their luggage.

Then going aboard, he went straight below.

It was Loelia who felt anxious about him and hurried down the companionway.

She knew instinctively that the cabin at the far end in the stern would be Lord Braydon's.

She expected that her cabin and her father's would be adjacent to it.

She went into the one on the left.

She found her father lying on the bed with his hand on his side.

To her horror she saw his fingers were covered in blood.

"Papa! Papa!" she cried. "What has happened to you?"

"They were suspicious about me," her father managed to say, through his pale lips, "and – somebody – stabbed me as I – left the station."

Loelia gave a cry of horror!

As she turned to the door desperately anxious to find help, she saw Watkins coming down the corridor.

He was without his cap but a mackintosh covered his gaudy suit.

"Papa has been stabbed!" she cried.

From that moment Watkins took charge.

He pulled off his mackintosh and the jacket of his suit.

He sent Loelia to fetch the Captain, who he said knew a great deal about wounds, and started to prevent Thurston Standish from losing any more blood.

Later, when she remembered all that had occurred Loelia was to think it was like stepping back into a nightmare.

It was Lord Braydon who ordered the yacht to sail immediately.

Instead of heading straight out to sea however, he set course down the coast towards Calais from where it was the shortest sea-crossing.

"If your father needs a doctor, which Watkins appears to think at the moment is unnecessary," he said to Loelia, "we could quickly put in to port along the coast, and it is also most important to save him from being buffeted about by a rough crossing for any longer than is absolutely necessary."

He spoke calmly and confidently.

Loelia was not so foolish as not to be aware that in her father's emaciated state, to lose a lot of blood from his wound might prove fatal.

Watkins came back from attending to his patient and Lord Braydon sent her out of the cabin.

She was sitting miserably in the Saloon when he joined her again.

Although she was not crying, he knew only too well what she was feeling.

He sat down beside her on a sofa covered with a very attractive English chintz.

He put his hand over hers and said quietly:

"It might have been much worse. If it had happened while we were still in Germany, we might none of us have been able to escape.'

"D . . do you . . think it will . . kill Papa?" Loelia asked in a whisper.

"Both Watkins and the Captain say that he was very lucky. The knife did not pierce any arteries, so it is not a really complicated wound."

He spoke reassuringly.

As Loelia looked at him to make sure he was telling her the truth, he saw the tears running down her cheeks.

Without thinking he put his arm around her.

"It is all right," he said gently. "I promise you that Watkins will save your father as he has saved me in the past. He is a natural nurse and was undoubtedly one in his last incarnation."

He looked down at her face against his shoulder.

He could feel her whole body quivering as if shaken by a tempest.

"You have been so brave up to now," he went on, "and we cannot let the Germans win at the last moment."

"Papa is . . all I have!" Loelia said in a voice he could hardly hear. "Th . . there is . . no one else . . no one in my life . . but . . Papa."

She felt as she spoke as if she was standing alone in a great void.

Then she suddenly became aware of the strength and comfort of Lord Braydon's arm.

He was holding her against him.

His hand still covered hers as she clenched her fingers together in an effort at self-control.

It was then she knew that when Lord Braydon left her, she would miss him.

She would miss him just as much as she would miss her father.

. . . .

"I've bin thinkin', M'Lord," Watkins said as he laid out Lord Braydon's evening-clothes, "an' I thinks that knife-thrust were meant for me!"

"What makes you think that?" Lord Braydon enquired.

"Well, I don't think they was aware that Mr. Standish had taken me place," Watkins said, "but they thinks I might 'ave something to do with 'is disappearance, so just on the chance, they gives me one, so to speak to remember 'em by."

Lord Braydon could understand the somewhat twisted reasoning by which Watkins had reached this conclusion.

He thought it was just like the Germans to revenge themselves without having anything substantial to justify it.

He was quite certain that by now the whole of Berlin was being ransacked in an effort to find Thurston Standish.

He decided they had not seriously thought that he and his valet had anything to do with Standish's disappearance.

If they had they would undoubtedly have made a greater effort to detain them.

"Do you think Mr. Standish will be all right?" Lord Braydon asked, deep concern in his voice.

"We'll have to feed 'im up, M'Lord, and make sure he loses no more blood, then he'll be as 'right as rain'."

"I hope you are right."

"Leave 'im ter me," Watkins said cheerily. "At the same time Your Lordship'll understand there's no question of moving 'im for a few days at any rate."

"I thought that is what you would say," Lord Braydon said. "So we will stay quietly on the coast of France before we cross the Channel and get back to normality."

Watkins grinned.

"That suits me, M'Lord. I like the 'Froggies', though I can't say the same about them Germans!"

Lord Braydon laughed.

He felt at the moment that Watkins was echoing his own feelings.

When he was dressed he went up to the Saloon.

He found Loelia waiting for him.

She was wearing a pretty but plain silk dress that was more suitable for the afternoon than the evening.

It was, however, the only gown she had besides the one in which she had travelled.

It was of pale blue silk, which not only became her but made her look absurdly young.

Once again Lord Braydon felt that he was dealing with a child.

At the same time he was aware how sharp and intelligent her brain was.

As he came into the Saloon looking exceedingly smart in his evening clothes Loelia looked at him with a little glint of appreciation in her eyes.

"Papa is sleeping peacefully," she said. "I peeped in at him, and Watkins told me that he had a whole bowl of nourishing soup before he went to sleep."

"I am certain," Lord Braydon said crossing the Saloon, "that we can leave your father in Watkins' capable hands, and try to enjoy a short holiday free from all our cares and woes."

"You are . . quite certain," Loelia asked in a low voice, "that you should not . . go straight . . back to England? I am sure they must be . . missing you . . and you are . . missing all the . . Balls and excitements of the . . Season."

Lord Braydon sat down on the sofa before he replied:

"When I was sent on that mission to Germany, I resented having to miss all the social events which you have just described.

"Now I feel quite content to be where I am."

His eyes twinkled as he added:

"But of course it will be your duty to make sure personally that I do not miss any other sort of entertainment."

He was teasing her, but Loelia looked worried as she said:

"How can you possibly suggest that I can even begin to . . compensate for all those . . pleasures you must be missing . . especially your horses."

"I had a feeling we would get back to horses sooner or later," Lord Braydon said, "and as we are at the moment anchored off a part of France where I know there are several racing-stables, I think we might arrange that you and I can exercise ourselves during those times when your father is asleep."

He saw the excitement sweep away the worry in her eyes before she said:

"Do you really mean that? It would be . . wonderful for me . . but you realise I have no . . riding-habit?"

"Then we shall have to send Watkins shopping once again," Lord Braydon said. "It is something he greatly enjoys and I must remember to compliment him on the choice of what you are wearing now."

Loelia looked down at the dress as if she had not really noticed it before.

Lord Braydon wondered how many other women of his acquaintance would have really forgotten what they were wearing.

And not thought of it the moment he came into the room.

"I am sure it is far more . . expensive than anything I could . . afford," Loelia said, "so . . please . . you must not spend any more . . money on me."

"That is something I have no intention of discussing," Lord Braydon said. "Everything you possess has been left behind in a place we may not mention, so you must allow me to see that until we return to England you are at least decently clothed."

"I . . I am sure I could find something . . cheap in which to ride," Loelia said.

"And I am equally sure that it would gravely displease Watkins, who rather fancies himself as an arbiter of fashion!"

Loelia laughed as if she could not help it, then she said:

"It is so much easier for me to say . . thank you very much for everything . . than to try to oppose you once you have made up your mind."

"Now you are being sensible," Lord Braydon said.

"Do you always think it sensible when you get your own way?"

"Of course!" he answered. "That is what I expect, especially when we are both engaged, as you well know, on a mission of great importance."

Almost as if he felt he must spell it out to her he said:

"Do not forget that you and I, and of course Watkins have rescued one of the most important men on the Secret File of the Foreign Office. I know that the Marquess of Salisbury will be delighted with us, even if he cannot publish to the world how clever we have been."

"You mean *you* have been!" Loelia said.

Impulsively she put out her hands towards him.

"If only I could tell you how much it . . means to have Papa with us . . and that he is . . alive."

Her voice broke on the last word.

"We are both going to have a glass of champagne,"

Lord Braydon said quickly, "to celebrate what is indisputably a great and resounding victory! I only wish we could have seen the Commander's face when he found the door locked, but that his 'bird had flown'!"

"It is quite obvious that he will suspect you and Watkins," Loelia said in a low voice.

"He may suspect us, but he will find it very difficult to prove even to himself that we are directly involved."

He poured out two glasses of champagne from a bottle standing on a side-table.

"It means of course that your father cannot go back to Germany again," he said, "and it would be definitely unwise once you are back in England, for you to do so."

Loelia gave a little cry of horror.

"You do not think . . you cannot imagine . . that the Germans when they . . learn that Papa has returned home . . will . . hurt him?"

There was a pause before the word 'hurt'.

Lord Braydon was aware that Loelia was thinking they might actually kill her father.

It was something he had already considered himself.

As he put the glass of champagne into Loelia's hand, he sat down again beside her.

"Now listen to me, Loelia," he said. "I have already thought about this, and I am going to suggest that for a while, or at least until we know the Germans are not interested in your father any longer, you both come to stay with me at my house."

Loelia stared at him in sheer astonishment.

Lord Braydon knew that it had never struck her for one moment that they might ever be his guests.

"Of course we cannot . . do that!"

"I do not see why not. You told me you had seen photographs of my house, and you must therefore realise it is large enough for any number of guests."

"But they . . would be . . your friends."

"Are you suggesting, after all we have been through, that you and your father are anything else?"

He saw the flush that crept into her cheeks.

She looked away from him shyly as she said:

"I like to think we are friends . . but it means . . something different from those you know . . ordinarily."

"Something very different," Lord Braydon agreed.

He then rose to his feet as the steward came into the Saloon with the first course of their dinner.

. . . .

The following morning, after ascertaining that his patient had passed a comparatively comfortable night, Watkins went ashore.

When he came back he found Lord Braydon sitting on deck in the sunshine.

He informed him that two horses would be brought from the small fishing-village about a mile down the coast from where they were anchored early in the afternoon.

He had also managed to procure a riding-skirt and a blouse for Loelia.

"There's another town about two miles away," Watkins said, "an' I'll go over there tomorrow or perhaps later this afternoon to see what I can find. Miss Loelia'll be quite comfortable in what I've bought her, and look very pretty in it, too."

He gave his master a glance that was slightly impertinent.

Lord Braydon ignored it.

"Thank you, Watkins," he said. "You had better show Miss Loelia what you have bought for her, and make sure that your patient has something nourishing for luncheon."

Watkins was quite unabashed by his Master's somewhat indifferent manner.

He hurried down to the cabin to find Loelia.

She, if nobody else, would be interested in hearing of the difficulties he had experienced in finding her anything suitable in . . as he put it . . 'such a God-forsaken place'.

After an excellent luncheon, Loelia, wearing the white

blouse with lace inserts and the wide skirt of some cheap but pretty material, went ashore.

When she was mounted on a well-bred horse, she could only think she was the luckiest girl in the whole world.

Watkins had been unable to buy her a hat, so she had instead pinned her hair very closely to her head.

Then because she was excited she forgot about herself.

She thought that Lord Braydon rode exactly as she might have expected him to do.

He seemed to be part of his horse.

Also it was impossible not to admire the stallion that Watkins had managed to hire for him.

They set off across the wild, uncultivated land which edged the coast.

Then they rode into a fertile valley with men and women working in the fields.

It was quiet and peaceful after the noise and turmoil and fears of Berlin.

Loelia thought that it was difficult to realise the two places were on the same planet.

Watching her face, Lord Braydon asked:

"Are you happy?"

"I was just thinking that I have stepped into a fairy-tale and that all my wishes have come true."

"Thank you," he said.

She laughed.

"And of course you are my Fairy Godmother, or I suppose it should be 'Godfather', except that he never seems to play a part in any fairy-story."

"I am almost afraid you will cast me in the role of the wicked Baron, or perhaps the Demon King!"

"How could you imagine such a thing? Of course you are Prince Charming. . ."

". . who discovered that the 'Goose-girl' was really a Princess?" he asked. "That would certainly be an achievement."

She looked away from him as she said:

"It must happen so many times . . or perhaps all your . . Princesses have always been . . Royal?"

"I thought you were part of a fairy-story," Lord Braydon said quietly, "and in my books the Princess was never cynical or sarcastic. She always looked at life 'through rose-coloured spectacles' and was therefore very happy."

Loelia drew in her breath.

"That is what I . . want to be," she answered, "but I am still . . afraid."

"I told you the goblins are all behind us," Lord Braydon said, "and I refuse to believe you are afraid of me."

"No . . only of . . waking up."

He laughed.

The warmth of the sun was cooling a little and the shadows were beginning to grow longer under the trees.

They rode back to the yacht.

As they saw the 'Sea Lion' lying in the small harbour, the sea very blue beyond it, Loelia asked:

"How soon will it be before Papa is well enough to return to England?"

"Are you in such a hurry?" Lord Braydon asked.

"No, of course not! I am only . . frightened that you will be . . bored and resent that we are . . imposing on you in . . this way."

"As I am extremely selfish," Lord Braydon said, "I would never allow myself to become bored. In fact, if I were, there is nothing to stop me from ordering my yacht straight back to England and once there leaving you while I return to what you have described as 'my amusements'."

"Is that what you want to do?" Loelia asked.

"I have already said that I always do what I want, unless I have received a Royal Command to visit Berlin."

Loelia laughed.

"At least the Prince of Wales cannot order you anywhere at the moment since he has no idea where you are!"

"That is just what I am enjoying," Lord Braydon said, "so stop trying to tempt me with what you think I am missing."

"Is that what you think I am doing?" Loelia asked. "But you are wrong . . of course . . I want to stay and . . ride with you . . talking to you is the most exciting thing I have . . ever done."

Lord Braydon did not speak and after a moment she said:

"I did not believe there was a man like you in the whole world."

"What do you mean by that?" Lord Braydon asked.

"You are . . young and yet you are so . . wise that you might be . . very . . very old. You are part of the social world and yet . . unless you are an . . outstanding actor . . you have enjoyed riding alone with me . . this afternoon."

She spoke not as if she was particularly wishing to compliment him.

She was just working it out in her own mind.

"I am prepared to agree with all that," Lord Braydon said. "And what conclusions have you come to about me?"

"That you are . . unique and very . . very wonderful!" Loelia said lightly.

Then her eyes met Lord Braydon's.

It was impossible for either of them to look away.

CHAPTER SEVEN

Lord Braydon walked into Thurston Standish's cabin and found him sitting up in bed writing.

"How are you this morning?" Lord Braydon asked.

Thurston Standish smiled at him and said:

"Will you sit down, My Lord. I want to speak to you."

"I rather anticipated that," Lord Braydon said, "but I thought I was wise to leave you alone for a few days until you had recovered from your stab wound."

"It is much better," Thurston Standish replied, "and before we go any further – here is my report on the gun in which you are interested."

He handed Lord Braydon some papers which he took from him.

At a quick glance he saw they contained exactly what he wanted to know.

"May I take these papers to the Prince of Wales?" he asked, "and let him present them to the Marquess of Salisbury?"

He spoke a little tentatively, feeling perhaps it was a breach of communications.

It was the Marquess who had sent Thurston Standish to Berlin in the first place.

"Considering that you saved me and my daughter," Thurston Standish replied, "I could not be so churlish as to deny you anything you wish."

Lord Braydon did not answer.

He was looking at the papers and thinking how delighted the Prince of Wales would be.

He would have something concrete to report to the Marquess, and to be undoubtedly 'first to know'.

"You know how grateful I am," Thurston Standish was continuing, "that you not only brought me out of Berlin, but saved Loelia from the dreadful consequences of her impetuosity."

"I hope you have not been very angry with her," Lord Braydon said quickly. "She is very conscious that she made a mistake, and it is something that will never happen again."

"Not, at any rate, as far as I am concerned," Thurston Standish said quietly.

Lord Braydon looked at him and he explained:

"This will be my last mission and, thanks to you, it has been a successful one. I had no wish to make my exit on a disaster!"

"I do not understand."

"Then I must make it clearer," Thurston Standish said. "I am, although no one except my doctor has any idea of it, a very sick man."

Lord Braydon looked surprised and he continued:

"When I left England, what I had been told by my doctors made it clear to me that if I was unable to bring back the plans of the German gun in which the Marquess of Salisbury was so interested, it would not matter to me personally because I should not be here to know that I had been a failure."

Lord Braydon still did not understand, though he did not say anything.

Thurston Standish however was aware of his perplexity and explained:

"I have tuberculosis and one lung is already badly damaged. As you will know, My Lord, it is only a question of a comparatively short time before I die, and the doctors have been frank and said there is nothing they can do to save my life."

"I am sorry . . desperately sorry," Lord Braydon said sympathetically.

"Do not be sorry for me," Thurston Standish said, "if I am prevented through ill-health from doing the things I really enjoy – and I suppose, if I am honest, danger is the breath of life to me – then I would much rather be dead."

He spoke quite calmly and naturally, and Lord Braydon said:

"I think in a way I can understand what you are feeling."

He was thinking as he spoke of the small Manor House and the few acres of land which Loelia had described to him.

He knew that was a constricted life under which he himself would chafe, let alone somebody who had roamed the world as Thurston Standish had.

"What I am going to do," Thurston Standish said firmly, "is to finish my third book, which is almost complete, then place it with the other two in your hands."

He looked at Lord Braydon pleadingly as he went on:

"If you will permit me, My Lord, to make you my Executor you can publish them whenever you think it is safe to do so. I know you will see to it that Loelia receives any money they make."

"Of course I will do that," Lord Braydon replied. "I can only say, Standish, how much you will be missed, and what a remarkable man you have shown yourself to be with your exploits described to me only in whispers and behind closed doors."

Thurston Standish laughed.

As he did so Lord Braydon looking at him realised that he was indeed a very ill man.

It was doubtful if he would live long enough to finish his book.

He glanced down at the precious papers that he was to take to the Prince of Wales before he said:

"I have a suggestion to make which I hope will meet with your approval."

Thurston Standish lay back against his pillows as if he suddenly felt tired.

He waited, and Lord Braydon continued:

"By this time the German Secret Police must be aware you have the secret of their new gun and will be looking for you, determined that you will not live to explain it to anybody."

Thurston Standish drew in his breath but he did not speak.

"I therefore suggest," Lord Braydon said quickly "that while you are finishing your book you stay here on my yacht."

There would be no need to elaborate to Thurston Standish what this would mean.

He would be free of wondering if he was being followed.

Of fearing every night when he went to bed that somebody would enter his room and kill him.

Above all, of knowing that to walk in the streets was to invite murder at the hands of what appeared to be a harmless passer-by.

"I have it all thought out," Lord Braydon said, "and my yacht can take you anywhere you wish to go. Personally I should think somewhere in the sunshine would do you more good than anything else."

He smiled as he added:

"A trip to the Mediterranean would certainly be enjoyable at this time of the year."

"It is something I would greatly enjoy," Thurston Standish replied, "and if I could choose where to lay my bones, it would be in Greece."

"Then my yacht is at your disposal," Lord Braydon said, "and you can leave me to look after Loelia."

"That is what has really been worrying me," Thurston Standish exclaimed. "I have two older sisters and several cousins who would be prepared to take care of her."

He sighed before he went on:

"But I think she would feel that life with them would

be extremely dull and very restricting after all we have been through together."

"I promise you I will look after Loelia and your plans."

He rose to his feet saying:

"I am now going riding with her, and when we return I shall order the yacht to take us to Folkestone. I am very anxious to see the Prince of Wales and know these plans are safely in his hands before there can be any chance of their being stolen from me."

"I certainly hope that will not occur," Thurston Standish said. "I could write them out again, but it would be a considerable effort."

"Leave everything to me," Lord Braydon smiled.

Having left the cabin, he went up on deck where Loelia was waiting to go riding with him.

She looked like Spring itself in a new green habit that Watkins had bought for her in the nearby Town.

Despite being made of cheap material, it had a French *chic* that with a riding-hat to match made her look very lovely.

"Watkins has again been impersonating Frederick Worth," Loelia laughed, "and I hope his choice meets with your approval."

"You look very smart and very French," Lord Braydon replied, "but you will have to buy a very different habit before you appear in an English hunting-field."

"I am afraid that is something that will never happen, for the Hunts have always been too expensive for Papa and me. But I am sure the few horses we have at home will be entranced at my appearance!"

She spoke teasingly.

Lord Braydon was just going to answer her in a different manner, then changed his mind.

Instead they went riding far into the French countryside.

They stopped at a small wayside Estaminet for luncheon where the food was delicious.

They talked animatedly during the meal.

When they set off to return to the yacht Loelia thought she had never in her whole life enjoyed herself so much.

Also, never had she been with a man who was so intelligent.

At the same time he teased her and made her laugh as if they were the same age.

When they arrived back at the yacht a groom was waiting to take the horses back to the stables where they had come from.

"You must say good-bye to our mounts, Loelia," Lord Braydon said, "for we shall not be riding them again."

Loelia looked at him.

For a moment he thought there was almost a stricken expression in her eyes before she said:

"I am very . . grateful to them for . . carrying me so well."

He lifted her down from the saddle.

As he did so he felt a little tremor run through her.

He paid the man for the horses before they walked down to the bay where the yacht was waiting for them.

When they went aboard, Loelia immediately ran down to see her father.

As she reached his cabin Watkins came out of it to say quietly:

"Mr. Standish is asleep, Miss."

"Then I must not disturb him," Loelia said. "Did he eat a good luncheon?"

"He tried, Miss, an' this afternoon for a little while he worked on 'is book, but I thinks the effort tired him."

"He must not do too much," Loelia said firmly.

As she went into her own cabin she wondered how he would be able to stand the crossing from the French coast.

Then there would be the journey either to Lord Braydon's house or to their own.

She had wanted to discuss it with him, but she had felt it would be a mistake for him to be worried.

She had decided therefore to wait until he was really well after his stab wound.

Now she felt herself beginning to worry.

Watkins had said he was better, but she was aware that he was still very weak.

He had not lost the terrible pallor that had shocked her when she first saw him in Commander Edersnier's cellar.

She thought Lord Braydon would prefer to be by himself after they had been together all day.

When she had taken off her habit she lay on her bed to rest before dinner.

She would have preferred to go on talking to him.

Everything they said to each other seemed so witty and sparkling.

She knew she must treasure those moments of being with such an intelligent man.

She had not really taken seriously Lord Braydon's suggestion that she and her father should stay at his house in Oxfordshire.

They must not impose on him any more than they had done already.

But she knew that to leave him would be an agony she dared not contemplate.

Lying in her comfortable cabin as the sun was sinking outside, she found herself praying that she might be with him for just a little longer.

When he was no longer there, her world would be very small and very lonely.

'I expect Papa will soon go off on another mission,' she thought. 'Then there will be nothing left for me but the horses and my anxiety as to whether Papa is in danger.'

She felt herself shiver at the idea that even before he went on a new mission, the German might still be trying to kill him because he had learnt too much on his last investigation.

'What shall I do? Whom shall I ask for help?' she questioned.

Then as the thought of Lord Braydon came to her as if in a blinding light, she knew he was the only person she could trust, the only person to whom she could turn for help.

"But how can I go on bothering him?" she asked herself.

As she thought of how kind he had been, how strong he was, and how authoratitive when it was necessary she knew that he filled her whole world.

It was something she had tried not to face, but she knew she loved him.

'I love him! I love him!' she told herself.

She felt the cabin protected her because it was on *his* yacht.

The *'Sea-Lion'* was like a magical Palace because *he* owned it.

As she had said laughingly, he was 'Prince Charming'.

"While I am not Cinderella, the Goose-girl, or the Princess of his dreams," she whispered.

She felt the tears fill her eyes because it was so hopeless.

She was longing for the moon which would always remain out of reach.

"I love him!" she said as she dressed for dinner.

She was wearing a new gown that Watkins had bought for her at the same time as he had purchased her riding-habit.

It was very simple, but again had the *chic* that an English frock always seemed to lack.

It made her waist look very small.

With her full skirts billowing out she was like a flower.

She did not know that to Lord Braydon she was a white rose not yet in bloom.

He was waiting for her in the Saloon.

Because she now admitted to herself her love for him, she found it hard to meet his eyes.

She felt shy as she walked towards him.

The yacht was at anchor and there was no movement of the sea.

There was only the soft lap of the water against the side of the ship and the setting sun cast a dazzling glow through the port-holes.

To Loelia it was part of her fairy-story.

Lord Braydon rose at her entrance.

She thought that no man could look more magnificent or more impressive in his evening-clothes.

She was also aware of him as a man.

"Watkins told me he had provided you with a new gown," he said, "and I expect you know already that it is very becoming."

Loelia felt herself blush.

Then because it was something she felt she had to know, she asked:

"Is this our . . last night . . together?"

"I hope not," Lord Braydon replied, "but that is something we will discuss after dinner."

The stewards were already bringing in the meal.

Just as they had done at luncheon, they talked on subjects which Lord Braydon could never remember discussing with a woman before.

Because Loelia had spent so much time with her father and also had read an enormous number of books, he had difficulty capping her quotations.

Also he had to strive to think up plausible arguments on some of the subjects she introduced.

It was all very fascinating, and when the dinner was over Loelia went below to say good-night to her father.

He was very sleepy and she did not stay with him for long, but went back to join Lord Braydon.

He was not in the Saloon but out on deck.

He was looking over the open sea which still had a touch of gold from the last rays of the setting sun.

He was standing at the rail and she went to stand beside him.

For a moment he did not speak, but only looked at her.

Once again, afraid to meet his eyes, she turned her face away.

"This is our last night here," he said after what seemed a long silence, "and I am wondering, Loelia, if you have been as happy as I have these past few days."

"You have really been .. happy?"

"Very happy."

She gave a contented little sigh and said:

"I was so .. afraid that you might be .. bored."

"I have always found in the past," Lord Braydon said, "that boredom comes from the obvious, and especially from knowing what the person one is with is about to say."

He paused and when she did not speak he went on:

"You have been very original and very different ever since I first met you."

"Thank .. you."

"I was wondering if, after we have been so close to each other in so many difficult situations, whether you will miss me."

His words hurt her because they implied they would soon be parted.

For a moment she contemplated telling him how desperately she would miss him and how without him nothing else could ever be the same again.

Then she thought that would be embarrassing for him, and looking out to sea she said:

"Of course .. there will be .. other things to .. interest you .. but I shall .. never forget how .. kind and how .. clever you have been and how .. wonderful."

"Do you mean that?" Lord Braydon asked in his deep voice. "I would like to believe that you are speaking the truth."

"But of course .. I am!"

"If I am to be sure of that, I want you to look at me, Loelia."

Because she was afraid he knew what she was feeling she continued looking out to sea.

Then as if he compelled her, without moving, without speaking, he made her obey him, she turned her head slowly.

Even more slowly she raised her eyes to his.

Then for a moment neither of them could move.

To Loelia it was as if there were only two grey eyes that seemed to grow larger until they filled the whole world.

Slowly, as if he was afraid he might startle her, Lord Braydon put out his arms and drew her close to him.

As he did so, he could feel the tremor that ran through her.

Then she was close against him.

He knew that her whole body was trembling, but it was not with fear.

He looked down into her face, her eyes very wide and questioning, her lips parted.

Her expression seemed part of the sun itself.

Then his lips were on hers, holding her captive.

To Loelia, it was as if she had stopped breathing.

The whole world was ablaze with the light of the sun which came from Lord Braydon.

She knew his kiss was what she had wanted, what she had longed for, but thought she would never know.

She had been unable to put it into words even to herself.

She knew the reason why she had been so happy, why it had been so wonderful to be with him, was that she was his completely.

Now there was nothing except the strength of his arms, and an ecstasy that seemed to seep through her body as if the sun swept through her.

Only when Lord Braydon raised his head did she say in a rapt little voice that did not sound like her own:

"I . . love you!"

She spoke almost unconsciously.

Lord Braydon found it impossible to find the words to say what he felt.

He therefore kissed her again.

Now there was a touch of fire in his kiss.

It seemed to Loelia as if the sunshine within her turned to flames and burnt their way from her breasts to her lips.

It was so rapturous, so unlike anything she had ever known or dreamt of, that she felt she must have died.

She was in Heaven – a Heaven of such ecstasy and wonder that the glory of it could never be expressed.

She could no longer think but only feel as she had never felt before.

Lord Braydon's kisses had carried her up to the moon which had always been out of reach.

The stars were twinkling inside her and the sun was burning like a flame.

She gave a little murmur and hid her face against his neck.

His arms tightened around her before he said unsteadily:

"I love you, my darling! I was so afraid to frighten you more than you were frightened already, but now that you love me, everything is 'plain sailing'."

"I love . . you! I love . . you!" she whispered.

"I want you to tell me that again and again until I am sure of it. I was so afraid you would not think I was clever enough for you."

Loelia gave a choked little laugh, as she said:

"How could I . . have been so . . foolish? Why did I not . . realise there was a man . . like you in the . . world?"

"I am here, and I will not have you looking for anybody else."

"As if I would . . want to!"

Then, as if Loelia was quite certain she was dreaming she looked up at him to ask:

"Did you . . really say you . . love me?"

"I love you until I can think of nothing but you, and we are going to be married as soon as we reach harbour on the English side of the Channel."

"M . . married?"

She found it hard to say the word and Lord Braydon said quietly:

"It is usual, my precious, when two people love each other."

"But . . I never thought . . I never dreamt that you would . . want to marry me! You are too . . grand . . too . . important . . perhaps I shall . . fail you . . then you will be . . s . sorry."

Lord Braydon laughed, and it was a very happy sound.

"That is a risk I must take," he said, "but I think it very unlikely, my lovely one, that we will ever be bored with each other, unless of course, you find being with me dull and unexciting after the life you have lived with your father."

"How can you . . say anything so . . foolish?"

Then she realised he was laughing at her and she added:

"Please . . I want to marry you . . but I feel it is . . something you . . should not do."

"Are you suggesting that, despite what we both know we feel for each other, I should leave you?"

Instinctively, Loelia moved closer to him.

She held onto the lapel of his evening-coat as if she was afraid he might vanish.

"I could not . . bear to lose you . . now."

"It is something which will never happen."

"But . . suppose . . just suppose the Germans . .?"

"You are not to think about it!" he said sharply. "In England we will be well protected and I have already made arrangements for your father so that he will be completely and absolutely safe . . ."

Lord Braydon nearly ended the sentence by saying: "for as long as he lives."

But he knew it would be a great mistake to increase Loelia's fear for her father by telling her that his days were numbered.

Once she was his wife and he could protect and look after her, she would understand.

Because she was so intelligent, she would realise that Thurston Standish would wish to die at the zenith of his career.

He would hate to grow old and find the exploits which he had enjoyed so much in his youth were no longer possible.

Loelia was soft and sweet, young and gentle and as Lord Braydon knew, unsophisticated.

He had sworn to himself that he would protect her and care for her, not only physically but spiritually for the rest of her life.

He knew that his first task was to make her so happy that when her father died it would not be the shock it would otherwise have been.

It would be something they could face together.

Their lives therefore would be enriched by thinking of him rather than be made miserable by regretting that he was no longer with them.

Lord Braydon said quietly:

"You will understand, my darling, that since your father with his usual brilliance has written down what he discovered about the secret German weapon, I am now obliged to take it as quickly as possible to the Prince of Wales."

His arms tightened as he continued:

"But as I cannot leave you, and have no wish to do so, I will take you with me as my wife."

"Are you . . sure that is the . . right thing to do?"

Loelia spoke anxiously, but at the same time Lord Braydon knew that no woman could look so radiantly happy.

Her whole face seemed to be lit by an inner light.

There was a radiance about her that made her more beautiful than anyone he had ever seen in his whole life.

"It is what we are going to do," he said. "In the meantime, because your father must be kept free of worry and of course out of danger, he is going to stay on the yacht and write the second part of his book."

Loelia gave a little exclamation of surprise before she said:

"Papa will love that! He adores being at sea, and I know he will be happy aboard this lovely yacht. Above all I shall not have to worry about his being pursued by the Secret Police."

"You are not going to worry about anything once you are married to me," Lord Braydon said, "except, of course – me!"

"I shall try to look after you," Loelia said, "and more than anything else I shall love you . . love you with all my heart and . . soul. Will that be enough?"

There was just a touch of anxiety in her last question and Lord Braydon said:

"You know that is what I want and what I have always lacked in my life."

He was looking at her as if he would impress her beauty on his mind for all time as he said:

"It would be foolish to pretend to you, my darling, that women have not loved me in their own way, but you are the only woman who has prayed for me, and has read my thoughts, and gives me something I have never received before."

"What is . . that?" Loelia asked.

His lips were very close to hers as he replied:

"I knew when I kissed you just now that you gave me not only your heart, but your soul."

"And you give me the sun . . the moon . . the stars, and the light which I know . . comes from God," Loelia whispered.

Then Lord Braydon was kissing her again.

Kissing her with possessive, demanding kisses which gradually became more passionate.

She was not afraid.

She knew now that love was not just the soft romantic emotion she had thought it would be.

It was something far more exciting.

It was as strong and vigorous as Life itself.

It could be as quiet and gentle as the sea lapping against the yacht, but also as strong, tempestuous and violent as a storm.

She knew Lord Braydon had a great deal to teach her.

Already every nerve in her body responded to him in a manner that she had never dreamt possible.

She knew that what she had found was love in all its strength and majesty.

He kissed her and went on kissing her as if he must make sure that she was his and he had won her for all time.

She said in her heart:

'I love you . . I love you . . and not even . . death can . . part us.'

. . . .

Lord Braydon's yacht was safely anchored in the harbour before Loelia awoke.

She had gone to sleep, thinking her whole world had changed.

She was no longer herself but somebody who was part of the man she loved.

She had no thoughts or feelings that were not his.

It had been very late when finally she left Lord Braydon.

It was later still, or rather early in the morning before she had gone to sleep.

She knew now that the sun was high in the sky.

Then she wondered if her father was worrying about her.

She got out of bed and put on a pretty cotton negligée which Watkins had bought for her and went into her father's cabin.

He was sitting up in bed writing, and as she came towards him he said.

"I have been told, my darling, that this is your wedding-day!"

Loelia made a little sound that was indescribable and ran to put her arms around him.

"Oh, Papa, I am so . . happy!"

"And I am happy for you, my darling," he said. "I think Fate has brought the right man into your life, and I know indisputably that you each belong to the other just as your mother and I did."

"I am sure that is true," Loelia said, "but you know, Papa, I cannot lose you. So, as Lord Braydon suggested, when you are better you must live with us at his house in Oxfordshire."

"For the moment I have a great deal to do," Thurston Standish said, "and as I shall do it better and quicker if I am alone, I have accepted your future husband's kind offer of his yacht."

He smiled and went on:

"I intend to visit places on the Mediterranean in a rather different style from which I have been accustomed to in the past!"

Loelia laughed.

"You will certainly be very grand with a private yacht rather than travelling as we did last time we were in France in a very uncomfortable carriage which was packed with other people."

Thurston Standish laughed.

"That was an adventure which I must remember to describe in my book!"

"You must also remember to include me, Papa," Loelia said. "You are undoubtedly going to be famous when your books are published, and I want to be a part of it!"

"A very large part of it!" he answered.

She kissed him.

After this they talked of what he would do when he finished his cruise on the yacht.

A little later she went to her room to dress.

She found there a very pretty white gown lying on her bed.

Beside it lay a wreath of orange blossom and an exquisite and, she was sure, expensive veil of Brussels lace.

She guessed Watkins had been busy again.

She thought it extraordinary that he should have such good taste where she was concerned.

When she was dressed she somehow knew she should wait until she was sent for.

She therefore knelt down by the bed to pray that her husband would never be bored with her.

She prayed too that their love would be as strong and beautiful as it was now for the rest of their lives.

'You will have to help me, Mama,' she said to her mother. 'I know how happy you were with Papa, and how well you looked after him, and I want to be the same.'

She was praying so intensely that she did not hear the door open.

She was unaware that Lord Braydon was standing just inside it looking at her.

He had not expected to find her praying.

He thought once again that of all the women he had known, Loelia was different.

So very different, that it seemed incredible that he had been fortunate enough to find her.

The intensity of his feelings communicated themselves to her even through her prayers.

Loelia turned her head to look at him.

Then she jumped to her feet and ran towards him.

He caught her in his arms and kissed her, not passionately, but very gently, as if she was infinitely precious.

She knew he was dedicating himself to her for all time.

"Everything is arranged, my darling," he said. "There is a carriage waiting on the dock which will take us to the Church."

Loelia could hardly take in what he was saying.

She was overwhelmed by the love she felt for him.

She looked at him and he said:

"How is it possible you are more beautiful every time I see you?"

"That is what I . . want you to . . think," she smiled, "and every time I see you I . . love you more than I did five minutes . . before."

Because there was no answer to this he kissed her, then hand-in-hand they went in to her father.

Loelia kissed him, Lord Braydon shook him by the hand, and somehow there was no need for words.

They were all three of them attuned to looking beneath the surface and finding what they sought within the other person.

As far as they were concerned, it could all be summed up in one word – love.

. . . .

Afterwards, Loelia thought her wedding-day was very different from what she had imagined it might be.

She and Lord Braydon were married in the little Church by the Quay-side.

It was hung with fishing-nets and was where the fisherman's wives, she learnt, prayed for the safe return of their men, when they were at sea.

It breathed an atmosphere of faith and love.

Loelia knew she would not have found that in any of the Churches in London.

Once they were married, with the Vicar's blessing ringing in their ears, they went back to the yacht.

There was a light luncheon waiting for them and after that a carriage took them to the train.

To Loelia's delight there was a special coach attached to it.

It would take them to the nearest station to Lord Braydon's house in Oxfordshire.

She had never been in a private coach before.

Lord Braydon watched her as she explored it like a child who had been given a new dolls' house.

"It is very exciting!" she said as she sat down beside her husband in the Drawing Room.

It had been arranged with comfortable sofas rather than with single armchairs.

"It is exciting because I can be alone with you, my darling."

"That is what I want, too," Loelia cried. "I think I shall be frightened when I have to meet a lot of people who will be wondering why you married me."

"They only have to look at you for them to find the answer to that!" Lord Braydon said. "At the same time, my precious one, you and I have a thousand answers which are very different."

He moved a little closer to her and she asked:

"Tell me . . what they . . are."

He looked down at her and there was an expression on his face that nobody had ever seen before.

"I love you," he said, "not only because you are beautiful, for your beauty is not just in your features which are perfect, in your skin which is translucent, or your eyes which are like stars. It is a beauty, my precious, which comes from your heart and soul, both of which belong to me."

Loelia gave a little cry of delight, then she said:

"I love you not only because you are handsome, but also because to me you are the cleverest man in the world . . and at the same time the kindest and the most . . understanding."

He was moved by what she was saying and knew it was not just a compliment.

It was a statement of what she really believed, he kissed her until the carriage seemed to swim around them.

Once again they were in a world of their own . . .

There was nothing except love and a blinding light which came from within themselves.

. . . .

Because she was so happy, Loelia was not upset by the great size of Lord Braydon's house.

Nor the army of servants who greeted them on their arrival.

Having been already informed of their marriage, the Butler made them a little speech welcoming Loelia and wishing them every happiness.

Because Loelia could read their thoughts she knew they were not thinking of Lord Braydon as an awe-inspiring master.

The older members of the staff were remembering him as a little boy whom they had watched grow up and had loved him almost as if he was their own son.

She shook hands with them all.

Then as Lord Braydon drew her up the stairs she looked at him enquiringly.

"I feel we are both tired after a long journey," he said, "and therefore I have arranged tonight that we will be informal."

He put his arm around her shoulders as they walked down the passage and he said:

"I have ordered dinner in your *boudoir*, and all you have to do is to have a bath, then wear a negligée which I am sure Watkins has procured for you."

Loelia laughed.

"I suppose one day I shall be able to choose my own clothes," she said, "but I am beginning to feel that Watkins will do it far better than I can!"

"I have every intention myself of giving you the most marvellous trousseau a bride ever possessed," Lord Braydon said, "but you will have to wait, my beautiful one, until we go to London."

He smiled as he added:

"Until then Watkins will procure anything you need, and as he spent a long time in Folkestone this morning, I think he will have found for you most of the necessities."

Loelia laughed again.

She was sure that nothing like this had ever happened to any other bride.

She was not surprised when having bathed in scented rose-water she found an exquisite nightgown waiting for her.

It was inlaid with lace and had a silk negligée to match in the soft pink of a musk rose.

"How could Watkins have found anything so pretty or so beautifully made?" she asked the Housekeeper who was helping her.

"Mr. Watkins informed me, M'Lady, that the finest sewing is done by Nuns.

"He therefore bought some of the lingerie you've been wearing from a Convent in France."

Loelia laughed.

It was all so fantastic that everything that happened was part of her fairy-story.

She was sure this was true when she entered the *boudoir* next to her bedroom to find her husband waiting for her.

He was wearing a long dressing-gown which was frogged with braid.

It looked almost like a military uniform, and she felt in her negligée that she was the one who was being unconventional.

However, because she was used to being unselfconscious, she soon forgot her shyness.

A table in the centre of the room was set with gold ornaments, gold candelabra, and decorated with orchids.

"We are going to wait on ourselves," Lord Braydon said, "or rather, I am going to wait on you, my darling, I felt we would not wish to be disturbed by servants or even be aware there is anybody else in the house except for ourselves."

Loelia thought that only he could think like that.

But before she could tell him so, he kissed her then poured out champagne for them both.

"A toast, my precious one! To us, and our love, which will endure and increase all through eternity!"

"That is what I am . . praying will . . happen."

"It will!" Lord Braydon replied and kissed her again.

She never knew what she ate or drank.

Everything seemed enchanted, and when dinner was

over Lord Braydon led her back into the beautiful room in which she had undressed.

Now the curtains were drawn.

There were only two candles burning beside the huge gilded bed with its canopy of cupids carrying garlands of roses.

Loelia thought Lord Braydon would take her towards it.

Instead he went to the window and pulled back the curtains.

Outside the moon was rising over the trees in the Park. The stars were coming out like diamonds in the sky and were reflected in the lake like points of fire.

The moon shone silver on the leaves of the trees and made the shadows under the trees seem dark and mysterious.

Then as Lord Braydon's arms went around her Loelia said:

"It is so lovely and exactly the right .. background for .. you."

"It is also a background for our love, my beautiful wife, and I hope one day our children will love it as much as we do."

The thought made Loelia blush.

She turned her head to hide it against his neck.

"I have .. something to .. tell you," she said very softly.

"What is it?"

She hesitated and feeling her quiver he said:

"I am waiting."

"When you found me in that .. terrible place," Loelia faltered, "I think I .. understood why men like the Baron went there .. for amusement .. but I am afraid you will think it very ignorant of me .. because .. I am not exactly .. sure what happens when two people .. make love."

Lord Braydon's arms tightened.

He knew as his lips touched Loelia's hair that this was something he never expected to hear from the woman he married.

He was used to associating with sophisticated married women with whom he had had so many *affaires de coeur*.

It had never struck him that a young girl would be completely innocent.

He had adored Loelia for her purity, and he had wanted to protect her because she was alone and involved in danger.

Now she fulfilled all his dreams in that she would only know about love from what he had taught her. It would be the most thrilling experience he had ever known in his whole life.

"Suppose," Loelia said, still in a very small nervous voice, "that when you . . love me . . you are . . disappointed?"

Lord Braydon held her closer still as he said:

"That is impossible!"

"Why?"

Instead of answering her he picked her up in his arms and carried her to the bed.

He undid her negligée and lifted her up again to lay her against the lace-trimmed pillows and cover her with the monogrammed sheets.

Then he went around to the other side of the bed, took off his robe and got in beside her.

He put out his arms to draw her closer to him.

He felt her quiver against him and it gave him sensations he had never known before in his life.

He desired her with a burning fire rising inside him.

At the same time what he felt for Loelia was utterly and completely different from what he had felt for any other woman.

"You asked me a question, my adored one," he said, "and now I am going to answer it. I could never be bored with you, because you are mine and because I not only love your beauty, your exquisite body and the sensations you arouse in me when I kiss you, but there is so much more!"

"Tell me . . please . . tell me," Loelia begged.

"First I love you for your sharp, intelligent, clever little brain."

He kissed her forehead before he went on:

"Then I love the affection you have for your father, and the way you think of him rather than yourself."

He smiled as he said:

"I have never known anyone so unselfconscious, who does not worry about her looks or what she is wearing, but concentrates on things that are really important."

"It was only when I . . loved you," Loelia said, "that I was . . afraid I was not . . pretty enough for . . you."

"By that time," Lord Braydon went on, "I was in love not only with your face, but with your heart and, as I have already told you, my angel, your soul."

He moved his lips over her cheeks and his hand was touching her body.

"They are all things that now belong to me, and so precious and so very, very exciting, my darling, that it would be impossible for me ever to be bored!"

He looked down at her by the light that came from the candles shining behind the curtains of the bed.

The moonlight which was beginning to encroach through the windows made everything seem magical and unworldly.

He could not help fearing that what he was about to do might frighten Loelia.

Yet, as if it was difficult to put into words he merely said:

"You must not be frightened, my sweet, because I will be very gentle with you."

Now Loelia looked up at him happily as she asked:

"How could I be . . frightened of . . you? I adore you . . I know too that I . . worship you. I would only be frightened if you . . no longer . . loved me."

"As that is impossible," Lord Braydon said, "we need only concern ourselves with our love, and it is love, Loelia, which makes me long for you to be mine."

Loelia moved a little closer to him.

"Please .. teach me," she begged, "teach me not only to love you in the way you .. want to be loved .. but how to keep you .. loving me."

She had no chance to say any more for Lord Braydon's lips were on hers.

Then he was kissing her with the demanding fire she had felt in him before.

She knew it was the strength and also the wonder of love.

She could feel his lips igniting flickering flames within herself.

He had no need to teach her because her whole body responded to his, as their thoughts responded to each other's.

It was so natural and at the same time so perfect that it was what they both wanted.

"I love .. you!" she whispered. "I love you .. until my love .. fills the whole .. world!"

"And I adore and worship you," Lord Braydon said hoarsely. "You are mine – mine, my darling – and I will never lose you!"

Then as the fire seemed to burn through them both and carry them up into the starlit sky, Lord Braydon made Loelia his.

A Divine Light covered them and swept them up towards the stars with the ecstasy which is the perfection of love and comes from God.

Coming next in your collection of
The Romantic Novels of
BARBARA CARTLAND

WANTED: A WEDDING RING

On her fifty-sixth birthday, Rosie Rill, all alone, looks back on her life. She had eloped with Vivian Vaughan, a music hall artist, who had then left her for a rich widow.

Rosie became a great success at the Gaiety Theatre, then fell madly in love with the Marquis of Colthaust. However, he will not marry her because he does not consider her blood to be as good as his.

As the memories of the past come crowding in on her, there is a knock at the door and Rosie is told that her niece, Ina, wishes to see her.

It is a shock to realise that Ina, at eighteen, is exactly like she was herself at that age, very beautiful and very innocent.

Ina asks for help as she is penniless, and suddenly Rosie, who, before her elopement had been Lady Rosamund Ormond, thinks of a way in which she can revenge herself through Ina.

How Ina is taken to Monte Carlo, how she meets the Viscount Colt, and how Rosie finds an old admirer, is all told in this enchanting new novel by Barbara Cartland.